WATER

A Cal Jamison Mystery

by Linda Kuhlmann

This novel is fictional. The names, characters, events, and places in this novel are products of the author's imagination or are used fictitiously. Any similarity to real persons, living or dead, is coincidental and not intended by the author.

ISBN: 978-0-9858333-5-0
ISBN-13: 978-0-9858333-5-0

Cover Design by Patricia White
Images used under license from Shutterstock.com

Other Books by
Linda Kuhlmann

The Red Boots

Koenig Triple Crown Series
Koenig's Wonder
Koenig's Spirit
Koenig's Promise

Cal Jamison Mystery Series
FIRE

ACKNOWLEDGMENTS

In writing this fascinating story, I received assistance from so many people that it is impossible to name them all. To everyone, I express my deepest thanks.

In addition, I would like to express my gratitude to the following people for their expertise, help, and encouragement. Although the final responsibility for the accuracy of the text is mine, I could not have completed this novel without these special people: Dr. Jana Van Amberg; Colonel Eric Thompson; Jeff Perin; Jantina Lowe, Judie Braaten; Anthony Lanuza; Ron Black; and Anthony Yanez.

Finally, a special thank you to my husband for his infinite patience and support.

PROLOGUE

A MEDIUM-HEIGHT MAN with dark hair and a large scar on the left side of his face stood at the JFK International Airport Customs counter. Christmas decorations were everywhere, even though the holiday was over.

"You just arrived from Afghanistan?" the U.S. Customs agent asked as he looked through the man's bag.

"Yes," the man answered impatiently.

The agent read the name and checked the photo on the passport, then he looked at the man. "What were you there for…Mr., huh, Iron?"

"Business." The man looked at his watch and added, "I have another plane to catch."

Then, amongst the man's belongings, the agent noticed a bracelet of what looked like red beads with a black dot on each end. "What is this?" he asked as he held it up.

"A gift for…my niece."

The agent smiled, returned it to the bag, and handed the papers back to the traveler. "Welcome home."

THE MAN TOOK HIS bag and walked into the terminal. 'Iron' was one of many aliases he went by in his business. He found the first handicapped restroom, went inside, and locked the door.

He opened his bag, pulled out a sealed envelope from a false bottom of his bag, and tore it open. He laid the contents on the counter near the sink. He smiled when he saw the small pocket knife, something he'd kept for over ten years. Then, he found the plane ticket for Red Cloud, Nebraska, and set it next to another passport, which revealed a different face than the one staring back at him in the mirror.

He hated it when he failed to finish a mission, but this time he wasn't just here to finish a botched job – this was his chance to get his own revenge on one last old score to settle. Anger rose as his eyes traced the long, ugly scar that ran down from his left eye to his jaw.

Inside the bag was a smaller one containing various makeup equipment and supplies. As quickly as he dared, he began transforming himself into the man in the second passport. He was a very patient man, which was vital for his job. And, his past theater experience years ago came in handy when a mission required this type of disguise. He looked down at two photos also in the folder. He noted the names of the two men who were his assigned targets.

The best adhesive he found to hold the costume prosthetic like the one he was applying to his face had a bit of flesh color. The process was like the reverse of a snake shedding its skin. This time, he was reapplying the discarded flesh. When finished, he looked at his new face and smiled, pressing down any loose edges with liquid latex to make a seamless finish down his neck and under his shirt. In less than ten minutes, the full-face and neck foam latex prosthetic had the desired creases and wrinkles he wanted and his mirror image now matched the new passport photo.

He changed into a plaid flannel shirt and khaki slacks that were too big for him. He quickly put on a gray wig that hung down to his shoulders and ortho shoes, then shoved everything into his bag. Checking his watch again, he donned a tan jacket.

The man smiled as he placed the beaded bracelet into one pocket of the jacket. The small bottle marked 'mouthwash' in his toiletry bag had gone unnoticed.

He stowed everything away into his bag, then put on the black gloves he always wore to hide his skin.

Correcting his posture in the mirror to imitate the façade he had created, the older man unlocked the bathroom door and walked out toward the terminal with the Nebraska flights.

CHAPTER 1

CAL JAMISON WAS IN his room at the Double J Ranch in Tumalo, Oregon. He'd been living at his grandparents' home since his medical leave the prior year and was now packing to return to his base at Camp Lejeune.

The Double J Ranch consisted of acreage to support his herd of twenty Belted Galloway cattle and a few Kiger mustangs Cal's grandfather had adopted from the Steens Mountain area of Oregon. The ranch was located northwest of Bend with a spectacular view of the Three Sisters, Broken Top Mountain, and Mount Bachelor.

Glenn and Winnie had built the log home in the early '90s. The rustic walls reminded Cal of his childhood home on a larger ranch not far from there, but like his grandfather, he still had issues with the rest of the Jamison family.

Cal had planned to leave after New Year's, but a quick change in the temperature boded for a heavy winter season, which happened a lot in elevations over three thousand feet. He was dreading this trip, not only because he would be flying in dicey December weather, but because of what he was about to do.

With his Marine uniform and cover packed, he opened the top drawer of his dresser to get more long-sleeved shirts. He stopped as his eyes fell on the photo of him with four of his teammates in their Marine Combat Utility Uniforms while on duty in Afghanistan. The photo was taken before they'd left on their last mission in the Helmand Province - before the IED blast that changed all their lives. The faces of three of his friends who died that year stared back at him – as if asking why that incident had happened. It was still unanswered after all this time and Cal didn't know if he would ever get closure.

The fourth face in the photo was Angel Ramirez, smiling with his buddies. But Cal knew that Angel was not smiling anymore. He had disappeared from his hometown in Colorado after the incident; and even though Cal had reached out to him many times, Angel never returned his calls or letters.

Cal was the commander of their Marine Special Operations Team. They were stationed in the Sangin District and his team shared the battle space with the 3rd Battalion 5th Marine Regiment, also known as the "Darkhorse" Battalion. They were there to train members of the Afghanistan National Army to use weapons for their own defense. The ANA were taught RPGs, M-240B Medium Machineguns, and AK-47 Assault Rifles. They also had locals who helped around the base and in the mess hall. One of these locals befriended Cal's team.

On that fateful day, Cal and his team were on a village stability operation, doing a patrol with Afghan partner soldiers. His immediate team was checking a school to ensure the Taliban was not trying to interfere. He was outside of the building with Angel, securing the perimeter while his other men were around the back. Matt, Paul, and

Ted were the first hit when the blast went off. They didn't survive the explosion. When Cal got to Angel, he was screaming in pain - his lower right leg was missing and blood was gushing from the wound. Cal had taken shrapnel in his upper body, but he still tried to stem the blood until the medics arrived.

That incident was why he was home on medical leave. He'd appreciated his physical therapist's recommendation to his CO to give him an extended leave, mostly because of the holidays, but now that time was over. Cal's CO expected him to re-up soon. He rolled his right shoulder, still feeling the effects of his injuries. The long scar that ran down his back pulled a bit. The pain was subsiding, but he still didn't have full motion yet.

The wind outside his window howled, bringing Cal back to the present. He shook his head as if to remove the horror of that day from his mind, but he knew it would never leave him in peace. He went to the window, pleased to see that it hadn't started snowing yet. His lifelong friend, Micco, was clearing the grassy runway by the hangar where Cal's Cessna waited.

Micco and Cal were born the same year on the Jamison homestead, a twenty-thousand-acre ranch near the Crooked River, north of Glenn's ranch. Micco's father, a cousin of Cal's grandmother, was the foreman of the larger ranch. When Cal's grandfather had a stroke the prior year, his friend had agreed to join Cal at the Double J to help with the chores on the ranch.

He turned and looked at each leg of his new flight plan on his iPad next to his bag. Originally, he'd created a direct path. Cal knew that flying alone across the country in winter had its challenges, but this weather had changed his mind. Because of the cold front moving through Central Oregon, he'd decided to take a more southern route to

North Carolina, knowing it would take him longer. His first leg was to Reno and then Arizona before heading east toward New Mexico. He'd meticulously planned each fuel and rest stop along the way on the Foreflight app. On one leg, near Childress, Texas, he knew he'd have to avoid that small area of restricted airspace. Then he'd continue east through Arkansas and Georgia before arriving at his destination.

Returning to the dresser, Cal pulled out his black baseball cap he'd had since high school. He'd worn it generally when he flew his plane and decided to take it along this trip to remind him of happier times in his life. Then, he stopped. Angel's last address in Nebraska was lying there at the bottom of the drawer. At that moment, Cal decided it was time for him to visit his friend.

CHAPTER 2

THE WELCOMING SMELL OF pancakes wafted through the hall as Cal walked toward the kitchen. He smiled when he heard his grandfather's booming voice.

"These cakes are light as air, Winnie," Glenn Jamison said to his wife. "But I miss my egg yolks and bacon."

"Remember your doctor's orders," Winnie said sternly, but Cal could hear the love in her soft voice.

Glenn had just turned eighty on December 12th. He was a robust man for his age and he always boasted, *It's the Scottish blood in me veins.* But his heart was starting to fail him. Cal knew that Winnie was attempting to change some of his grandfather's bad habits as his doctor suggested. She tried to get him to limit his pipe smoking, but she wasn't always successful. Cal never understood why his grandparents insisted everyone call them by their first names, but he respected their wishes.

He set his bag and flight jacket near the front door and walked into the room.

"Is there any left for me?" he asked.

"Always," Winnie said smiling as she hugged her

grandson. "Good morning, dear."

She was a short woman with the high cheekbones of her Northern Paiute ancestry. Her hair hung in a long braid down her back, surprisingly still dark at her age with only a few silver strands on her left temple. She wore a flowing robe of many colors, which showcased her incredible artistic talent. Cal knew that she'd made the robe herself in the traditional patterns reminiscent of her tribe.

"Mornin', son," Glenn said, wiping his hands on his napkin.

"And a good morning it is." Cal kissed his grandmother on the cheek.

"Are you about ready for your long journey?" Glenn asked.

"I am." Cal poured himself a cup of coffee. He sat down at the old pine table across from his grandfather.

The kitchen was small but efficient with a new retro model of a 1930s chrome and enamel gas stove like Winnie used to have. It was more in the style of the log home. She opened the stove's warming compartment door.

"It's been so good having you home," she said as she placed a plate heaped with food before Cal.

"I'm just glad you were here for Christmas," Glenn said, running his hand over his aging red beard. "What a fine time that was getting out the old kilt and doing a few highland flings."

"I agree," Cal said smiling. It was one of the few times he wore his tartan kilt of the Jamieson Scottish clan.

When his ancestors first came to America in the early 1800s, their family name had been changed from the Gaelic 'Jamieson' to the current spelling. He was proud of their heritage that went back to the northwestern highlands of Scotland, near Connel Bay.

"It wasn't like the holidays of old at the homestead,"

Glenn said nostalgically as he looked out the kitchen window over the sink. "Those were some big shindigs - when all the family was together." He sighed, turned again to Cal, and said, "I wish you didn't have to go."

Cal knew his grandparents were dreading this, but he had decided not to tell them about his plans until he returned.

"What's next for the cattle?" he asked to switch the subject from his impending departure.

Glenn said as Winnie sat next to him, "Before this storm hits, your friend, Micco, and his cousin, Tocho, are going to help move the cattle to the shelter near the woods behind the barn."

"I wish I could help," Cal said, "but I need to fly out today. This winter weather is coming in fast this year."

"It's okay. You have a deadline with the military." Glenn took a sip of coffee and added, "Our new neighbor, Gabe McNary, just finished our last harvest before this first snow comes in, so we have enough feed for the cattle. He's one of Cecile's nephews on his mother's side and he's turned out to be a real nice guy. It was a shame when Cecile died, he was a good friend for many years." Glenn began to giggle. "I remember him telling me how he always hated his name because he was teased in school for having a girl's name. It was supposed to be Cecil, but the nurses made a mistake on his birth certificate. I always wondered why he never changed it."

"I met Gabe," Cal said. "I'm sure you appreciate that he's going to continue working your back forty alfalfa field and supply you with hay."

"Your brother, Jack, already called this morning," Glenn said. "He said he needs your input on some changes at the Jamison Ranch."

"He can wait," Cal said before he took a large bite of

pancakes.

"You're going to have to face him one day," Glenn said.

Cal and his younger brother didn't get along, ever since Jack swayed their mother to sell some of the old homestead property, which had been in the Jamison family since the early 1800s. Cal's father was killed near that area but the shooter was never found.

"Have you heard from Mary Creswell lately?" Winnie asked smiling. "She is such a sweet girl."

Cal met Mary earlier the previous, about the time her brother-in-law, Luther Greeves, was killed. Cal and Luther rode in rodeos together and became good friends. His murder had been devastating to the Creswell family, but Cal was glad he had been able to help solve that case.

"No, Winnie, I haven't. I think she may be going back to her job at the art gallery in Seattle soon."

Winnie frowned. "That's too bad. I thought maybe you and she had something going…"

When he didn't respond, Glenn smiled. "Watch out, son. Your grandmother is a matchmaker."

Cal stood, took his plate and cup to the sink, then hugged his grandparents.

"I'd better get going," he said. "I'll call to let you know when I arrive." He looked at the two special people in his life. "I love you."

"Love you, too, son," Glenn said as he and Winnie followed Cal to the front door.

Cal was surprised to see tears welling in the old man's eyes. He smiled, picked up his bag, hugged Winnie again, and walked out of the log house.

CAL FOUND MICCO IN his apartment above the large garage at the Double J. The two men had each other's backs since they were young and Cal totally trusted him with his life.

He hung his jacket on the peg next to the door, dropped his bag, and sat down on the couch. He wasn't surprised that Micco was already sitting at his desk, where he spent most of his nights doing some research on his computer. Unlike Cal, Micco's job in the military had been in the Communications Unit.

"I can't believe how fast this weather's changed," Cal said as he looked around the uncluttered space. The area was one large room but the kitchen was separated by an island. The bed sat off to Cal's right.

"Yes, I know it's changed your plans a bit, but you have to go," Micco said as he looked around the two large monitors on his desk.

"Yes, I'm flying south first."

"How long is it going to take you to get to North Carolina?"

"Three to four days with fuel stops and rest, but I might be gone a little longer. I have another stop to make."

"I think I know where."

Micco knew Cal's demons he fought with since he'd been injured. That's why he'd found his teammate's address in Nebraska for him, which is what he did best – finding lost things.

Cal nodded. "I need to see Angel."

"Yep," Micco said smiling. "I thought you might. Once you're in the sky, you can fly anywhere."

"You going to be okay here while I'm gone?"

"Sure, no problem. Tocho and I've got this covered. We'll let Glenn be in charge, but we'll do the heavy lifting."

Cal looked away, still feeling guilty. "I appreciate it," was all he said.

Micco got up and joined his friend on the couch.

"I've got something for you to sign," he said, handing Cal a file. "It's the final paperwork for your P.I. license."

Cal scanned the documents and looked at his friend. "Triple A Detective Service? Really?"

"It's great, right? The name puts us at the top of Google searches and a phone directory, for those who don't use the Internet."

Cal shook his head as he signed where Micco had placed Post-it notes.

"Have you told your grandparents about all this yet?" Micco asked.

"No, I want to wait until I get back." Cal leaned back and sighed. "This is going to be a big change for me."

Micco nodded. "You know I retired from the Marines last March. Sure, I miss my friends in the service, but I'm beginning to enjoy this new adventure in my life." He nudged Cal with his elbow. "I think you will, too. Heck, I may even have a case or two lined up for you when you get back."

CHAPTER 3

ANGEL RAMIREZ TOSSED AND turned in his small bed at the back of his mobile home in Red Cloud, Nebraska as the horrifying movie played in his mind. Sweat poured from his body, his dog tags stuck to his bare chest.

"We've got them all, Commander," he yelled out to Cal, "but we're in trouble."

The sand-filled images kept racing in his dream as he relived the events just before the blast that transmuted his life. Some soldiers were leading the children and teachers away from the school building while mortars exploded around them. Three of his immediate team were still inside. He and Cal had just stepped out when they were caught under fire.

Bullets flew past his helmet as he inched down the mud brick wall of the compound toward Cal. Out of the corner of his eye, he saw a shadow… Then, the earth shook and his body was tossed into the air. When he landed, he knew his leg was gone.

Suddenly, Angel awoke with a gasp. It was a dream he couldn't shake since that incident in Afghanistan. His team had been ordered on a village stability operation with Afghan partner soldiers, but this time, the memory of that day was different. He now had a face to the shadow he'd seen – the man who caused that blast!

He sat on the edge of the bed in his shorts and looked around in a daze, his dog tags now dangled from his neck toward the floor. He hadn't been able to remove them, even though he'd been given a medical discharge years ago. Paranoia and head trauma were some of the results of that blast, besides losing part of his right leg. He winced as he slipped on his prosthetic device on his lower stump. The leg was still red from his work yesterday at the feed store, but he tried to ignore the pain.

Angel limped to the front of the trailer and sat at the table near the small kitchen. His hands shook as he lit a cigarette, which was happening now more recently. He knew it was time to take his meds for his PTSD, but he had to finish this first. He grabbed a pencil and a piece of paper and made a quick note, then he sat back and stared at the name on the paper for a long time, the smoke of his cigarette rising into the air around him.

Knowing that Cal could be in trouble, he tore off another piece of paper and began creating the cipher, using the code for sensitive information Cal had created for his team. His commander would be able to figure it out, but somehow, Angel had to get the message to Cal as soon as possible.

He set flame to the first message and watched as it burned in the ashtray. He thought of how he'd pulled away from Cal to forget that day – yet he never could. Then, looking at his watch, he opened his laptop and searched for flights to Oregon. After he printed his trip info, he took his meds and dressed for work. Before leaving, he went to the back of the mobile home and placed the coded message in a safe place.

CHAPTER 4

EAST OF BEND, JAMIE Greeves stood on the porch in front of her white farmhouse that her father had built. He liked to call the place his Creswell Ranch, even though it was only a few acres. Two Black Angus cattle grazed in the small pasture, and the red barn stood to her right where they kept the horses. Jamie and her younger sister, Mary, were born there. After Jamie and Luther were married, she inherited the farm from her parents.

Duke, Jamie's dead husband's old coonhound, lay at her feet, his legs twitching as if he were chasing some prey.

She pulled her jacket tight around her in the morning chill and sighed heavily as tears streamed down her cheeks. She wondered how she was going to manage the land and animals – now that Luther was gone. He'd been a marvelous husband and father to their two kids, and a respected firefighter in Deschutes County. But Luther was murdered the previous year by a man she never knew. She also had something new to worry about.

The door opened behind her and she turned to see her sister. Mary wore a large down jacket over her usual colorful clothes.

"I can't wait to see the snow again," Mary said. "It mostly rains all year in Seattle."

"Yes, it is beautiful."

"The kids are finished with breakfast." Mary looked at her sister. "It will be good for them to get back with their friends after this winter break."

Jamie nodded. "We need routine back in our lives." She looked at her watch and said, "And, I should get to work at the courthouse." She kept the real reason she wanted to restart her life to herself.

Mary hugged her sister. "It's been so good being home again. I can only stay a couple more days or so, but then I'll have to go back home. My boss keeps emailing me."

"I am so thankful that you were here when all this happened with Luther. I don't know what I would've done without you. The people at the Raven Gallery in town will miss you, too."

"That's what sisters are for. Besides, the gallery people here knew I was only temporary. And, look at all the changes I've made to my art. I'm excited to get back to work."

"You have so many lovely pieces at the local gallery in town and they're selling quickly."

"I think I've actually found my true art media while I've been here." Mary ran her fingers through her long brown hair. "Winnie Jamison has been such a God-send in showing me new designs and materials for my paintings."

Mary stopped and looked at her sister. "Are you okay?"

"Why?"

"You just have that look on your face like when our favorite dog, Bentley, got sick."

"I'm fine," Jamie said.

JUST THEN, TWO CHILDREN came out of the house. Duke woke and slowly got up to greet them. Riley, Jamie's son, had turned seventeen a few days after his father died. He still refused to talk about it and spent most of his time in the barn with the horses – like he used to with his dad.

Josie, the usually bubbly, petite ten-year-old, was subdued and quiet. Even her bright pink coat did not add color to her small cheeks. She looked so much like her mother, Mary liked to call her 'Mini-Jamie.'

"Hi kids," Jamie said, attempting to lighten her voice. She smiled and hugged her daughter. "Aunt Mary's going to stay with you today."

"I'm bored," Josie whined. "I want to go to Susie Bond's house."

"Not today."

Josie stomped back into the house.

Riley scratched the dog's long ears and said, "I have rodeo training at the riding center later. Is it okay if I take Dad's truck?"

Jamie looked at Mary, then said, "Sure."

"Also," Riley continued, "my girlfriend, Olivia, wants me to go with her to the mall tomorrow, something about after-Christmas shopping. She probably just wants me to carry her packages."

"Maybe I'll take Josie today if that's okay with you," Mary said.

Sighing heavily, Jamie nodded and walked to her car.

CHAPTER 5

A TALL, SLENDER WOMAN in her sixties with long brunette hair and sharp green eyes was pacing in her office at the large Jamison Ranch. Nina was strong for her age because of the work she did when help was needed. On the mahogany desk, that probably came to the ranch on some ship decades ago, were papers and maps of the land of her dead husband's ancestors. She felt that she was running it all into the ground. The ranch was in Jefferson County and had grown with each generation to its current size.

She looked around the room at the Lodgepole pine walls of her 1910 house, the second that was built on the property since her eldest son's namesake homesteaded here and built his first cabin in 1820. Callum Jamison began as a fur trader from Scotland. Now, Black Angus cattle roamed the land and were the main source of income, but the ranch was losing money in the current economy.

Nina ran her hands through her hair as her second son, Jack, walked in and sat in the chair across from the desk. He had red hair that he inherited from his grandfather, Glenn. She'd relied on Jack for years now.

"You look troubled," her son said.

"What are we going to do now?" she asked as she sat in her chair.

"I have a plan." Jack leaned back into his chair, placed his hands behind his head, and smiled.

"What do you mean?"

"The land the old sawmill is sitting on is doing nothing to help us."

"But your great-grandfather built that mill."

"I know, but we no longer need it. I've been doing some research." He looked at his mother excitedly and added, "I'm still working out the details, so I'll need a little more time."

"I trust you, Jack. You've been my rock here…since Cal left."

Anger came into Jack's eyes. "He's being a total eejit for abandoning us like this."

She smiled at his use of the Scottish slang, but then said, "Cal's going through so much right now with his medical issues and Glenn's recent stroke."

Jack hated it when his mother covered for his older brother. He stood up and yelled, "He won't answer my calls. I've tried to include him in the business of THIS ranch, but he just doesn't seem to care anymore."

Sadly, Nina said, "He's going back to active duty in a few days… this last injury really scared me."

Jack sighed, went to his mother, and put his arms around her. "I know…me too."

After a moment, Nina shuffled a few papers into a folder and said, "How are your other brothers doing? Do they know about all this?"

"I haven't discussed it with them yet. Clyde has been a great help here on the ranch, but Tate spends most of his time now at the Redmond airport, working as an airplane mechanic." Jack sat down again and added, "Wes told me yesterday we're going to need more help here, especially with the kind of winter they're predicting. He'll know who to hire."

"That's going to require more money."

"I know," Jack said, "but I told you, I have a plan."

Nina thought of when her husband had hired Micco's father, Wes, as his ranch foreman. He was strong and very knowledgeable of the land and she had come to appreciate his help in more ways than one.

She nodded and said, "I'll talk to Wes about this later."

CHAPTER 6

AT THE MALL THE next day, Riley followed Olivia from store to store as they fought their way through the crowd of people. He hated shopping for this reason, especially since he'd been right about being her bag boy. But there was one particular store he needed to visit while he was there.

Olivia was about to go into another shoe store. His girlfriend had a shoe fetish and took forever to make a choice.

Riley handed her the packages and said, "I'll be right back."

"Where're you going?" she asked as she fumbled with the bags.

"I have to pick something up. I won't be long." Riley quickly left her standing in front of the shoe store.

He walked down the wide hallway, trying to avoid the little kid with an ice cream cone that was coming right at him. When he got to the trophy store, he went in. Thankfully, it was one of the businesses that wasn't totally packed with people.

One day last week, Riley's mom had asked him to gather all the livestock records his dad kept on his desk in the barn. Going through his dad's things brought back so many memories of their rodeo days together. Numerous ribbons and buckles were in the front drawer from past events they'd won. That's where he found a receipt from this store at the mall.

"I'm Riley Greeves," he said to the clerk behind the counter as he handed him the piece of paper. "My dad brought in something to get engraved. Is the order ready?"

The blond man looked in his order book and smiled. "Yes, it's right here."

Riley's heart leaped in his chest when he saw the man pick up the familiar Barrel Racing Trophy with the gold horse, barrel, and rider on top. He'd gotten the award at the Sisters Rodeo the prior summer – the last rodeo he'd been to with his dad. It was an event that happened shortly before his dad's horrible death.

"This looks great," he said as he paid the man. "Thank you so much."

Riley stood outside the store as he turned the trophy over and saw his father's words engraved on the bottom of the base – *I knew you could do it, son!*

Tears came to his eyes as he started walking back toward the shoe shop, but he tried to hide them. He thought back to that race, of how Sherlock, his sorrel Quarter Horse, had excelled when he started him on the left barrel instead of the right, as his dad had taught him. All the other riders went in the opposite direction. Riley often joked with his dad that if his horse was a person, he'd probably be left-handed, like he was. He'd named his gelding after the famous English detective that he loved to read.

SUDDENLY, HE FELT AS if he'd walked into a brick wall. Riley looked up and saw Travis Moore, a bully from school who also rode in the Youth Rodeo program, but he wasn't very good at it. He had a small gang of mean boys that followed him everywhere and Travis' dad was a PE teacher.

"Awe, take a look at this, boys," Travis said, grabbing the trophy.

"Give that back!" Riley yelled, aware that all the other people near them were looking at him now.

Travis was taller than Riley and held the trophy up over his head. Riley jumped, trying to reach it, but then Travis broke it quickly over one knee. Riley got so mad that he punched the bully in the face. Travis then tossed the trophy pieces onto the floor and flew at Riley while all the other kids swarmed around the two boys as they fought and began cheering them on.

"Break it up!" an adult voice roared over the noise of the crowd. Everyone scattered, including the bully's other gang members.

The two boys stood frozen looking up at the mall security guard. He grabbed each boy by the collar of each of their jackets and said, "You're coming with me to my office."

Riley was glad when he looked back and saw Olivia pick up the two pieces of his trophy.

CHAPTER 7

KEN WHITAKER'S FAMILY HAD owned the feed store in Red Cloud for over thirty years. He was grateful to be able to continue his legacy. As he watched the men and women who worked for him, he felt a great sense of accomplishment. His dad and granddad would be proud of him, even if he'd made a few changes to take the store into the current century.

He looked at his watch and saw that it was getting close to lunchtime.

Angel Ramirez, one of his men who'd been working for him for six months, was a stocky, strong young man. But as Ken watched him handle one of the large bags of livestock feed, he noticed that he was favoring his right leg. Ken knew that Angel was in the Marines and had a prosthesis, but the younger man never gave up.

"You want to take a break?" Ken asked.

Angel turned to his boss and said, "No, I can manage." He set the heavy bag down and asked, "But I need some time off for a few days…I just have to get out of here for a while."

"How much time do you want?" Ken asked.

"I'd like to leave in a couple of days, I'm not sure how long – maybe a week?"

"It's pretty slow here now, so I don't think that'll be a problem." Ken looked around at the now-empty warehouse and said, "It's time for lunch. I had some burgers sent over from the Palace. I don't like eating alone, so would you like to join me in the break room?"

Angel stopped and took off his leather gloves. He pulled out a red handkerchief from his back jeans pocket and wiped his forehead, taking a moment before answering.

"Sure," the younger man answered. "I'd like that. But you have to let me pay you back."

"Deal."

THE TWO MEN WERE alone in the break room, which Angel appreciated. All the other workers had gone off somewhere to eat and the room was pretty sparse other than a couple of vending machines, and a sink over a small window overhead. The burgers smelled good and Angel realized he was very hungry. He took a pack of Marlboros from his shirt pocket.

"You can't smoke in here," Ken said as they sat at a round table.

"But it calms my nerves." Angel reluctantly put the pack away. "I keep forgetting about the new laws on public smoking. I was in Afghanistan off and on for six years - overseas for four to six months, then one year off to rest and train." He paused for a long moment, then added, "You could smoke everywhere over there."

"I know you came here from Colorado," Ken said, ignoring the military comments. "Why'd you end up here?"

Angel looked out the small window at the sky, then he

shrugged and said, "It was as good a place as any."

"Does your leg hurt very much?"

Surprised, Angel looked at his boss. He always tried to conceal the fact that he had a prosthetic on his leg ever since he started working there.

"I noticed you limping a few times," Ken said. "Don't get me wrong, you're one of the hardest workers I have, but I know when someone has an artificial leg."

Angel tried to smile. "I thought I hid it better than that. Am I going to be fired now that you know?"

"Heck no. I just don't want you hurting yourself – that's all."

For a while, the two men ate in silence.

Then, Ken asked, "How'd you get injured?"

"An IED," was all Angel would say.

The older man nodded. "I understand. But you never really answered my question about why you came here."

"I grew up in Silverthorne, Colorado. I was a big skier all my life—" He stopped and looked down at his leg. "That was before all this happened."

Ken watched as a shadow fell over Angel's face, but he remained silent.

"When I came home from the Middle East," Angel said, "people looked at me differently - even my own family…I just wanted to disappear - become a ghost."

"I know the feeling." Ken took another bite of his burger, then wiped his hands on a napkin. "Do you miss the mountains?"

Angel nodded. "Sometimes I do, but I found this great place west of Haigler, over in Dundy County. It's called Tri-Point, an area where three states come together. I also like to hike McCann Canyon, but it's not the same as Colorado."

Ken nodded. "I've been there." He knew what it was

like to want to disappear…

CHAPTER 8

AT THE DESCHUTES COUNTY courthouse, Jamie was researching some information on her computer. She was always interested in the technical field, but her commitment to her family right now was more important. Today, she needed to understand her future.

She found one site that had some information and jotted a few notes on a steno pad, then went to a different site. Jamie knew she could get in trouble for using a work computer for personal business. And she was beginning to feel overwhelmed with all the conflicting advice, but she was desperate to get some answers.

Jamie heard footsteps behind her, the familiar sound of thighs rubbing against pantyhose, which made her quickly close the website. Then, she hid the notepad under some files and began nervously shuffling papers on her desk.

"This just came in," her supervisor said, handing a red file to Jamie. "Top priority."

Lois was a large woman with big eyes and fat fingers. She always walked with one arm crooked as if she was carrying a handbag or preparing to wave to a crowd like a queen.

Jamie looked at the file and saw that it was an old cold case. She knew this case. It was a woman who had disappeared five years before.

"This is the Willoughby Case," Jamie said.

"Yes, I had just started here when that happened. Her body was never found and, like the DA, I always suspected the boyfriend for her disappearance but there was no proof."

Jamie nodded. "She was a school teacher." She looked at the newest report in the file and read the deputy's note out loud. "A week ago, a body was discovered near Mallard Marsh Campground by some people on horseback. The skeleton was identified as Joyce Willoughby, and the pathologist discovered a different DNA on some of her clothing."

"That's why it's being reopened," Lois said.

"It says here that a DNA test result of the boyfriend was taken when he was hired for a job at a college in the Midwest." Jamie looked up at her supervisor and added, "That was shortly after the time of the murder. I wonder if someone in our tech department is working on this."

"Yep, I knew he was guilty. Well, this is going to be a new one for the records."

"I know! Isn't it exciting? I just recently read an article in the newspaper about how DNA tests that were done by Ancestry for people looking for their ancestors or current relatives may help solve cold cases. Wouldn't that be something if we could find this woman's killer that way?"

"How do you know so much about this?" Lois asked.

"I read a lot," was all Jamie would admit to. "So does my son, Riley."

"You do love mysteries," the other woman said, shaking her head.

"I have all of Agatha Christie's books and read them every night before going to sleep. *Rebecca* is my favorite – it has a cold case that is solved." She didn't explain that she was also interested in maybe learning more about the technical evidence the courts were using.

The supervisor started to walk away, but Jamie stopped her.

"Uhm, Lois, I need some personal time off in a couple of days."

"What for?"

"It's personal."

Just then, Jamie's telephone rang. When she answered it, she was surprised to hear a man's voice asking her if Riley was her son.

CHAPTER 9

MARY STOOD BEFORE THE easel in the farmhouse kitchen. She preferred the studio in her apartment in Seattle, but this room had the best light for painting. She looked at the photo on the table next to her paints and mixed some Prussian blue pigment with a burnt umber combination she'd made to get a rich black for the horse she was working on. The canvas was almost finished but the horse's mane needed to be a deeper color.

At the table, little Josie was drawing on a small artist's tablet with colored pencils. "What color should I make my horsey, Aunt Mary?" she asked.

"What color do you want?"

"Pink!"

Smiling, Mary nodded and looked down at her own palette. She noticed that she was almost out of the umber pigment, which meant she would need to return to the Crooked River to get some more rocks. Cal's grandmother had shown her which rocks to use to get specific natural colors and how to grind them down for her oil pigments. An image flashed in her mind of a tall red-headed man she'd seen on her first visit to the Jamison Ranch…

Mary was so involved with her work that she was startled when Jamie came in the door with Riley. She looked at the clock over the stove and saw it was only two in the afternoon. Then, as Riley entered the house, she saw his red eye.

"What's going on?" she asked Jamie, putting her brush in a jar of distilled turpentine and wiping her hands.

"Riley did something bad," Josie said in a sing-song voice.

"Shut up, you squirt!" Riley yelled at his sister.

"He's grounded for a stunt he pulled at the mall," Jamie said.

"But I didn't start it and Olivia wants to go—" Riley started.

"You're not going anywhere, young man, now both of you go to your rooms."

Josie started to cry as she ran upstairs, "I didn't do anything…"

Riley glared at his mother and stomped away.

"What stunt?" Mary asked.

Jamie laid her keys and the broken trophy on the counter. She knew how much it meant to Riley, but with Luther gone, she knew she had to be firm.

"Some kid was bullying Riley and they got in a fight. The security guard at the mall was about to arrest my son, but I was able to talk him out of it. I argued that it was probably because the other kid had instigated it." She sighed and added, "That doesn't cover the fact that Riley was the one who threw the first punch."

"How long is he grounded for?" Mary asked.

"Only a week."

Riley came back into the kitchen.

"Where are you going, young man?" Jamie asked

sternly.

"To do my chores."

"I can stay with him this week while you work," Mary offered.

Jamie looked at her sister. "What about your job?"

"When I called yesterday, they said they had a new temporary person coming in to help with my shift. I'm sure it won't be a problem."

"I don't need a babysitter," Riley shouted and stormed out of the house.

Mary picked up the broken trophy and asked, "What's this?"

"Riley won that at a rodeo he and his dad went to last summer. He said the bully broke it and I'm sure that's what set him off, but it doesn't excuse his reaction."

"I have no idea how you do it, raising your kids, since I don't have any of my own. But you've done a wonderful job. These kids are a testament to that."

Jamie sat in the chair at the table. "I'm not so sure these days. It's been hard lately, especially with a teenage boy."

Mary went to her sister and put an arm around her shoulders. "Riley will be all right. He's just still hurting right now."

Jamie looked up with tears in her eyes and said, "We all are."

"Do you have to go back to work?"

"No, I called my boss and told her what happened." Jamie looked at the canvas and said, "Wow, you've been busy. That is beautiful."

"Thank you." Mary cleaned her brush on a rag and softly said, "This might not be the right time to ask, but would it be okay if I go to the Jamison Ranch sometime to get more rocks? I'm running out of pigments for my oil-based paints. I'd like to do it before this weather changes."

"You just said you were going to be here for Riley while he's grounded."

"I'll only be gone about an hour. I can do it later in the afternoon, a little before you head home from work. I don't think he's going to get into that much trouble till then."

"I guess that's okay." Jamie got up and went to the sink. She poured a glass of water and took a large gulp. She was about to tell her sister about her upcoming doctor's appointment but decided against it.

CHAPTER 10

CAL'S 172 SKYHAWK'S ENGINE hummed as he checked his location. He'd turned the bill of his cap around backward to give him more visibility. He knew he was flying over the Palo Duro Canyon in Texas toward KCDS, Childress Municipal Airport for a fuel stop. Looking at his flight plan, he checked his ETA and gauges. His first night was in Kingman, Arizona and he planned to continue now until arriving in Conway, Arkansas. He'd figured he should make North Carolina in two more days tops.

Since he wasn't flying on an instrument flight plan, traveling easterly, he had to fly at odd-numbered altitudes. He was restricted from flying above eighteen-thousand feet in his 172 since that is PCA – Positive Control Airspace. He knew that flying now could be risky, with short breaks between fair weather and icy conditions. But, so far, he'd had good luck and all was well.

When flying at cruising speed, his thoughts always wandered. He liked this time alone. But, sometimes, the solitude would stir up old feelings. Now, in his mind, he replayed the memory of the one woman he ever truly loved

– Sarah Leisner. They'd met in a camp in Iraq when Cal had been injured. She was a medic and the moment he looked into her green eyes as she tended to his wounds, he knew he was a goner. He'd survived his injuries, but when she was killed during an attack on their camp, a wall had surrounded his heart.

Shaking his head to release the memory, he looked at his playlist on his iPad that was connected by Bluetooth to his headphones. He searched through and found Keith Urban's "Little Bit of Everything." Cal thought that maybe it was time he started playing his own guitar again.

As the music played, he looked at the sky around him and saw beautiful cumulus clouds. He remembered a book he'd read by a man in Oregon about the various types of clouds. Being a pilot, Cal was always fascinated by these different formations. Luckily, he was still ahead of the front he knew was coming and the weather had held so far as he traveled east.

To kill time while flying, he liked to make out shapes in the clouds that resembled other things in his life, like the head of a horse or a lion's head. He'd even seen the famous "Green Flash" once when flying over the ocean along the western coast. It wasn't as brilliant as shown by Hollywood in one of the *Pirates of the Caribbean* movies, but he learned that if he didn't blink and waited for the sun to go just below the horizon, it would flash green as the bright star's flare shone up through the ocean's waters.

One time, when flying through dark clouds, he could swear he'd seen the face of the devil. He didn't believe in omens, but he knew there were forces bigger than what could be seen that shaped our world.

IT WAS GETTING LATE after Cal crossed over

Amarillo, Texas when suddenly his alternator light came on.

"Dammit," he exclaimed as he stopped the music. "I knew I should've taken time to switch out that old alternator before this trip."

In all the hours he'd flown before, this wasn't the first time something went wrong. He started his descent into Childress Airport. Cal knew there was an FBO there called Boedeker Flying Service. He hoped they'd be able to get a new part and change it out for him without too much delay.

Cal got on the radio and announced that he was fifteen miles to the west and inbound for landing. "Childress Traffic this is November 386MikeCharlie…"

After touchdown on Runway 36, he taxied his plane to the Boedeker's FBO on the east side of the runway. As he climbed out of his plane, he was met by abnormal balmy weather for Texas in December.

A mechanic came out of the maintenance building to meet him. "Hi, I'm Ralph Compton," the robust man in cowboy boots said as he wiped his hands on a greasy shop rag. "How's your plane running? It sounded like you wanted to get down quickly."

"Yes," Cal said. "I'm so glad you're still here. My alternator light came on."

The mechanic went back into the building and returned with a multimeter to test the alternator.

Ralph said, "Yep, you're going to need a new one. I can get a part to arrive early tomorrow morning. Why don't you go on into the office and talk to Sydnee about a place to stay for the night."

"That would be perfect." Cal gave him his cellphone number.

"Be careful though," the mechanic cautioned. "She's

single…"

IN THE OFFICE SAT a petite woman with long blonde hair and deep dimples when she smiled. She wore a leather teal blue skirt and vest over a sheer white blouse. He could see the outline of her pink bra underneath and knew he was in trouble.

"Hello, there," the woman said, giggling. "My name is Sydnee – like Sydney, Australia, but my mom spelled it with two 'e's."

"Hi, I'm Cal."

She got up and offered her hand, which Cal shook and quickly released. "I'm going to need a hotel for the night," he said as he looked down at her boots that matched her skirt. "Any suggestions?"

"I know a place near a great steakhouse." Sydnee quickly grabbed her purse and keys and said, "My shift just ended and I can take you there. It's only a few miles into town."

As they walked outside, Sydnee headed toward a green '50s Buick Super Station Wagon with pristine wood paneling. It even had the spot lamp still on the driver's door.

"Wow, that's a great-looking vehicle.," Cal exclaimed.

"Thanks. This was my dad's. He restored it a year ago, just before he died."

"I'm sorry to hear that. Uhm, is there a taxi or Uber service I can use in town to get a ride back here tomorrow?"

"Oh, sugar, I'd be happy to bring you."

CHAPTER 11

THE NEXT MORNING, CAL arrived early at the Childress airport office building with Sydnee. He'd seen the mushroom cloud approaching in the distance to the west and was hoping he could take off as soon as possible. He wanted to make one stop in Georgia, and then get to Camp Lejeune the following morning. The weatherman on the motel TV warned about severe weather coming in.

"In about an hour, this system will bring intense thunderstorms," the dark-haired meteorologist on the screen had said. "Because of unseasonable warm weather and lots of moisture coming up from the Gulf Coast, we will be experiencing lightning and heavy rains coming from a Mesoscale Convective System. These storm systems can reach thousands of feet in the sky and sixty miles wide."

Before he'd left the motel, Cal called the number for a pre-flight weather briefing on his route east. The meteorologist available suggested that he divert southerly about twenty degrees to avoid moderate to heavy precipitation.

The prior evening with Sydnee had been interesting.

She'd driven by the suggested Motel 6, then to the steakhouse. As a thank you for driving him, Cal decided to offer to buy her dinner. He'd figured he would be safe with other people around. Sydnee mostly talked about her living in a trailer across town with two cats, Ginger and Peaches. When their steaks arrived, she'd asked him questions about where he was from and what he did, which Cal vaguely answered - remembering Ralph's words. When she grilled him if he had a girlfriend, he'd only apologized and said that his heart was already taken.

Now, at the airport, Cal quickly got out of Sydnee's station wagon and said, "I appreciate the ride...and the company."

"Thank you so much for buying my dinner," she said smiling, wearing a red skirt and boots." I just wish we had more time together."

"Sorry, but I have to be on the East Coast in a few days."

"I love your stories about Oregon," she cooed hopefully. "I've always wanted to go there."

"Goodbye, Sydnee, and thanks again," he said.

AS CAL WALKED TOWARD the mechanic's shop, his phone began to ring, and the sound of a 1984 song by Wham! filled the air – *Wake Me Up Before You Go-Go…*

"Damn it, Micco," he exclaimed. His friend was always playing tricks on him and changing his cellphone's ringtone. But this time, as he crossed the asphalt, he listened to the familiar tune he and Micco used to sing sometimes while working at the Jamison Ranch when they were young. It almost made him want to start a little dance, but instead, he answered the call.

"You did it again!" he exclaimed.

"Ah, you like the new ringtone?" Micco asked.

"At least this time I know how to change it back. Is everything good at Glenn's?"

Micco paused, then said, "We're okay, a bit swamped with this snowstorm here getting feed to the livestock. I called Gabe McNary to come over. Where are you now?"

Cal felt remorse for not being there to help. Finally, he answered. "Texas. I had a mechanical problem, but I think I'll be in the air again soon. One more stop before I reach the east coast."

"It's good to hear your voice," Micco said.

"You, too. Tell everyone there 'Hello' for me."

"Roger that. Text me when you get to North Carolina. Make sure you call your grandparents, too."

"I plan to." Cal hung up.

He walked to the Boedeker building under the Phillips 66 sign.

The mechanic came out of the office and said, "Mornin', Cal. I got your part and it's already installed. Earlier, I did a quick flight to test it and you're good to go."

"You're a good man, Ralph."

After Cal had paid, the two men walked back to the hangar where the Skyhawk waited. He stowed his bag on the back seat.

"So, how was last night?" Ralph asked smiling.

"It was good, but I appreciate your advice." Cal looked back toward the office and saw Sydnee waving at him. He waved back and added, "She's a nice lady, but I've met many women before who were looking to marry a pilot."

"You dodged a bullet this time."

Cal didn't mention that his past would always get in the way of him ever getting close to another woman.

Ralph turned and looked at the cloud that was now a brilliant orange color because of the sunrise. "That thing is going to break loose in a while and could last for hours. You'd better get in the sky, buddy."

Cal thanked the man again. He climbed into the plane and did his usual preflight check. As he taxied to the end of the runway, he looked back at the towering cumulus that looked much like what pilots would describe as a 'mushroom cloud.' Then, he put on his Ray-Bans and took off toward the sun.

CHAPTER 12

THE MAN IN DISGUISE stepped from his rental car and looked around the sleepy town of Red Cloud. He was glad he'd bought a heavier coat and some boots at the airport, considering the snow on the ground. Few people, probably mostly locals, walked past the large red bank building that was built in 1883. Everywhere were signs about a famous author named Willa Cather who grew up there.

He walked to an old telephone booth and was surprised to see it was still operative. Thumbing through the directory, he smiled as he noted the address for Angel Ramirez. Suddenly, his stomach growled and he realized he hadn't eaten all day.

He spotted a nearby coffee shop and went inside. Only one couple was at a small round table, chatting over their lattes. A silver-haired guy sat at the counter, wearing a hat with a feed store logo.

The young clerk came over and took the man's order - a scone and black coffee.

"You new in town?" the guy in the hat asked.

"Just passing through," the man said shortly in a raspy voice. He didn't like to have people get to know him while he was on a job.

"Where you headed?"

Quickly, the man thought of one of his stories and a town he'd seen previously on the Nebraska map. "I'm on my way to see my niece. She lives west of here, in Haigler – near McCann Canyon."

"I have a friend, Angel, who goes there when he misses the mountains in Colorado, which is where he said he grew up." Reaching out a hand, the guy said, "I'm Ken Whitaker."

Thankfully, the man's order was ready. He ignored the silver-haired man's hand and said, "Have a nice day."

Outside, the man got back into his car without engaging with anyone else in town. He quickly ate the scone and put Ramirez's address in the GPS app on his cellphone. As he drove, he sipped the strong coffee.

THE MAN PARKED A distance away from Ramirez's trailer, which was at the end of the lane near some trees. He smiled when it began to snow. Looking around the mobile home park, the man stealthily went to the trailer and peered through a corner of a small window that looked into an empty small table and kitchen area. The place had few decorations or mementos that most people put up in their homes. It was neat and orderly. *Just like a Marine*, the man thought.

Then, the man ducked back as Ramirez walked up the hallway from the end of the trailer and went to the sink. The man watched carefully as his mark took some meds, sipping from a gray thermos near the sink to wash them down. He smiled, knowing how he was going to complete part of his mission.

As Ramirez stepped toward the door, the man hid in the trees and watched his target walk out and drive away.

The man looked around again and expertly picked the lock. Before he went inside, he slipped off his boots on the step and walked in, leaving no trace. With gloved hands, he quickly searched through drawers and cabinets without disturbing anything, looking for any information that could help him on his quest.

As he was about to leave, he noticed the ashes in the tray and Ramirez's laptop on the table. He expertly attached a device to the computer and hacked into his prey's email account. The most recent was a message confirming a plane ticket to Redmond, Oregon.

"That must be where Jamison is," the man said softly to himself. "Now the game begins."

CHAPTER 13

GLENN WAS IN THE barn at the Double J Ranch filling water buckets as Micco finished putting the hay bags in each stall for the Kiger Mustangs. The breed was started when Spanish Conquistadors brought them to Oregon in the 1500s, and an adoption program that began in 1986 runs every three or four years for private buyers to help preserve the wild breed.

"I can do more," Glenn insisted as he pulled his collar up around his neck against the cold. He was standing next to Bravo, Cal's stallion, scratching the white pyramid marking on the animal's dun-colored forehead. Five years before, Glenn adopted Bravo for Cal when he was home on leave.

Odie, the old black and copper Australian Shepherd, now came over to lay at Glenn's feet.

"That's the last bundle," Micco said as he wiped his hands on his handkerchief.

"Have you heard from Cal?" Glenn asked as he sat on a bale in the aisle.

"Yes, he was delayed for a day in Texas, but has one

more layover in Georgia before arriving in North Carolina."

"I know my grandson is a good pilot, but I worry every time he takes one of these long flights."

Micco smiled. "You know he is a highly skilled pilot and loves to fly."

"I just wish he'd call me sometime."

"I'm sure he will when he gets to Camp Lejeune."

"Thank you for your help," Glenn said and took out his pipe and tobacco pouch.

"You know Winnie won't like it if you smoke that," Micco cautioned.

"I know," Glenn said, putting only a small amount of tobacco in the pipe. "But it's the only time I can do it – when I'm out here."

Micco looked at the older man as he lit the tobacco and said, "Unless you need something else, I'm going back to my apartment."

"I'm good," Glenn said, smoke whirling up around his head.

ALONE IN THE BARN, nostalgia washed over Glenn as he looked around at the number of horses he'd helped to save. If the BLM didn't have that program, many of the Kiger Mustangs would die on Steens Mountain from starvation. He'd started breeding a few as a sideline for his cattle business.

Feeling vulnerable since his stroke, the old man was angry that he was not able to do the work needed on his ranch. The cattle were now protected from the snowstorm, but they still had to be fed and watered daily in this extreme weather. Also, he was afraid of how many cattle he may lose because of it. He began to wonder if he should start cutting down the size of his herd.

The tobacco in his pipe was out by now. He got up and walked to the door and knocked the cold tobacco out onto the snowy ground. Then, he tucked the green and blue tartan scarf Winnie had given him for Christmas tighter around his neck and turned to go back inside the barn.

Suddenly, Odie got up and started barking.

"What's up, boy?" Glenn asked as he quickly put his pipe in his coat pocket, afraid his wife would catch him.

Gabe McNary, his neighbor, walked in with a black lab wearing a vest. Even though Odie went up to the dog, the lab ignored him and remained by Gabe's side.

"Micco told me you were here," Gabe said. "How're you doing?"

Glenn looked at the younger silver-haired man who reminded him of the singer everyone called 'The Gambler.' "I'm okay," he said. "Are you getting settled in?"

"Yes. I was glad when Uncle Cecile gave me his ranch. I like living here much more than in New York."

"What did you do there?" Glenn asked.

Gabe decided not to mention his rich family's background on Long Island. "After I got back from Nam, I didn't really work much – mostly mowed grass at a local golf course. Then, I landed a great job at the agriculture office. I learned a lot about farming on the East Coast there."

Glenn sat down again and said, "You were in Vietnam? I had two sons who fought over there. They were both pilots. One came home, but one is still missing – probably dead by now, but I refuse to bury an empty coffin."

"I'm sorry to hear that."

"Why is Roscoe wearing that harness?" Glenn asked.

"He's a trained Service Dog and goes everywhere with me. He's been my best buddy since I got back." Gabe saw the look on the older man's face and explained, "I have, uhm, anxiety issues and he keeps me calm…" Scratching the dog's neck, he added, "Roscoe's saved my life numerous times." He didn't add that he had been a prisoner in a Vietcong camp for six years and had residual medical issues because of it. Nor did he mention he didn't fit in with his family's high society when he returned.

"Well, it's good you've got each other." Glenn rubbed his arms and said, "It's getting colder in here, why don't you come in for coffee."

"I'd love to, as long as Roscoe can come along. He's housebroken."

"Absolutely."

CHAPTER 14

CAL WORE HIS SERVICE uniform as he drove the rental car toward the Camp Lejeune Marine Corps Base. He tugged at the collar, surprised that he felt a bit strange after so many months on medical leave. The military was not only his job, but his life and he'd worn the uniform for twenty years. All that was about to change.

Earlier, he'd flown the last leg of his long journey from Habersham County, Georgia, just northeast of Atlanta, and landed at N22, the Sky Manor Airport located west of Jacksonville, just outside the Class D airspace of the military base. It was a small privately owned airport with a turf runway. He left his Cessna 172 there, changed into his uniform, and arranged for a rental vehicle.

The line of cars at the base was not surprising considering the morning traffic. As Cal drove up to the security gate, his orders lay on the seat next to him. After showing his ID to the guard, he was saluted before he drove on.

The familiar long road seemed endless as he dreaded what he was about to do, but he felt it was the right decision. As he passed some of the officer's quarters along the banks of the New River, he thought back to his Basic Reconnaissance training at Camp Pendleton. He smiled as he remembered the first time he rappelled a tall tower. His instructor had said 'Don't look down,' and Cal never forgot that advice. Then, after a deployment to Iraq, he was transferred to Camp Lejeune for training with the MARSOC Marine Raiders.

Green flags lined the drive to indicate weather conditions for outdoor activity. Cal knew that a black flag in North Carolina meant it was too hot and a possible risk of heat exhaustion. The base was like a large college town with everything a soldier could need.

THE MARINE CORPS BASE headquarters came into view. The Julian C. Smith Hall, a Colonial-style building, was built in the '40s and was once a Naval hospital. He parked in a spot near the door and was hit by the humidity as he stepped out of the vehicle.

Cal walked into the building. The walls of the wide entry were lined with photos of prestigious officers, both past and present. To one side sat an old Gatling gun mounted on wheels that he guessed probably dated back to the Civil War. He presented his ID to the man in uniform behind the counter and signed in. Then, he walked up the stairs and down the green-carpeted hallway to his CO's office. The door was open.

Looking in, Cal saw Major Walt Morrison sitting behind a large mahogany desk, his brow furrowed with concern as he looked at a file in front of him. The walls of the room were mostly bare except for a few photos of old units and plaques. There was an old map of Middle-Eastern countries on one wall to the major's left and a picture of his wife and daughters on his desk. Cal knew that the oldest daughter loved horses.

"Permission to enter, sir," Cal said.

"Enter," the major responded.

Cal saluted his CO and stood at ease as the older man looked up and smiled, quickly closing the file.

"Well, Cal Jamison. You're early," Major Morrison said as he stood. "You're not due back for another week."

"I always preferred to be ahead of time," Cal said, shaking hands with his commanding officer. "It's good to see you again, sir."

"Yes." The major motioned to one of the two chairs across from his desk. "Take a seat."

"Thank you." He looked at his commander he'd known for years and asked, "How's the family?"

"They're all fine, preparing for the New Year."

Cal knew that the major liked to fish, so he asked, "Have you been getting any fishing in lately?"

"Yes, I caught a twenty-one-inch Speckled Trout last weekend in the New River, even though it is brackish. I was using MirrOlure, a suspending twitch bait lure, with live mullet and shrimp. Cold weather doesn't seem to bother those babies. Did you get any fishing in while on leave?"

"It was part of my therapy," Cal said smiling. Then, as he eyed the file on the desk he added, "You look well, but it seems something's bothering you."

Major Morrison nodded. "I could never get anything past you." He pulled another file over the prior one and added, "I saw that your rehab time was extended. How're you doing? Are you ready to get back to work now? I could really use you."

Cal took a deep breath and said, "I'm okay, but I'm sorry to report that I will not be re-enlisting… You see, my grandfather's health is not good and he needs me now to help on his ranch."

The major sighed and leaned back in his chair. A clock on one wall ticked away in the silence. "I'm surprised and very sorry to hear this."

After a few awkward moments, the man said, "Cal, you are too valuable for the Marine Corps to lose you. Would you consider IRR – Individual Ready Reserve? It is an eight-year commitment for possible recall if needed."

Cal thought about that. He knew that even if he chose not to go into the Reserves, in time of national crisis, he could be recalled involuntarily. He shook his head and said, "I have to put my family first, sir."

The major nodded. "I understand."

Cal said, "Once I get back home, I'm also thinking of getting a Private Investigator's license as a sideline."

The older man smiled. "That sounds like you – multi-managing your life. And, your job in the Marines has prepped you to be a great detective."

Looking out the window for a moment, Cal said, "After losing my men in that attack last year, I need to make a change."

"Will you have time to visit the graves of your men at Arlington while you're on the East Coast?"

"Not this trip."

"Have you heard from your team member, Angel Ramirez?"

"Not since our return from Afghanistan, sir." Cal paused and added, "I lost track of him…but recently found that he's now in Nebraska. I'm going to see him on my flight home – if weather permits."

"I understand, son, how hard it is for some who come back wounded. Did you fly your plane here? How long did that take?"

Cal nodded. "Four days, with a mechanical issue in Texas, but you know I love to fly."

The major smiled.

Motioning to the files on the man's desk, Cal asked, "Have you had any more intel about the attack on my team?"

Major Morrison frowned, then said, "Yes, but I already have a team on it. And, since you will no longer be on active duty, I cannot divulge anything about it."

"But, sir, I know more about that event than anyone else—"

"I'm sorry, Cal."

AFTER HE LEFT THE building, Cal sat in his car, angry to be left out of the loop of information because of his decision. But eventually, he realized he was more upset at himself. He knew the chain of command and that he no longer had any business here.

He decided to do one last run around the base. As he drove along the river on his right, he replayed in his head his experiences here and the people he'd met over the years. He passed Marines doing exercises on the obstacle course.

He showed his ID again as he went through the gate to the MARSOC headquarters, his last area of training at the base.

Inside the headquarters building, Cal was met by a guard. He showed his ID again and then walked down the hallway – the memories flooded in his mind. He stopped where commemorative boards and mementos were hung by prior groups. One board in particular had photos of his platoon during their training and first year's deployment. The men and women were so young then with visions of the new part of the world they were about to see. None of them had any idea what was ahead of them.

As he was about to leave the building, the guard called his name.

"Master Sergeant Jamison, I have something for you."

Cal walked over and the man handed him a small box. "These things were left here by Lance Corporal Watson and I was told to mail them to you, but since you're here…"

In the car, Cal opened the box. On the top of a few items he'd left behind was a photo. The familiar face stared back at him, which took the air out of his lungs. It was Sarah in her operating room scrubs. He'd taken it with his phone when he'd been injured. He sat for a long time trying to catch his breath as the memory tore his heart apart. But then, he realized it was just that – a memory. He put the photo into his wallet.

As he slowly drove back through the gate where the words *Always Faithful, Always Forward* were marked in large bold letters, Cal knew he was going to miss the military. But the possibility of a recall someday, if his country needed him, inspired him to continue down his chosen path.

CHAPTER 15

JAMIE WAS SITTING IN the empty waiting room of the Bend Cancer Center. Colorful magazines littered the end table next to her chair, but she was not interested. She was glad she was alone so she didn't have to talk with other patients as her mind reeled with fear of what was in her future. Her first mammogram ever had revealed a suspicious mass in her left breast.

The first surgeon she'd gone to scared her to death with all the probabilities she was facing, including a full mastectomy. But she had asked for a second opinion. She'd learned early on regarding her and her family's health that it was okay to question a diagnosis and today, she was praying for a miracle.

"Mrs. Greeves," the receptionist said. "The doctor will see you now."

Jamie hadn't been called 'Mrs. Greeves' since Luther's death. She wished he was here to give her support as she stood and followed the woman to an examination room.

IT WAS COLD AND sterile in the sparse room, as Jamie sat on the edge of the long table. Even though she was petite, she pulled at the back of the cotton gown, wishing they had a little more material to go around her. She looked around the room and saw a certificate hanging on one wall from John Hopkins. Then she saw a framed photo of a family rafting down the Deschutes River on inner tubes and thought of how much fun it was when she and Luther used to take the kids there each summer.

After a short while, Dr. Dena Bello came in and extended her hand. "Good morning, Mrs. Greeves."

Jamie tried to smile as she shook the hand of the older black woman with blue eyes. She'd read somewhere that a mutated gene caused this anomaly in some people.

"Please, call me Jamie," she said. "I know I probably look like a deer in the headlights to you, but I've had the bejesus scared out of me by one surgeon already, so I only want to know what I need to know at this time."

The doctor smiled, looking at Jamie's file. Then she said, "I understand."

Dr. Bello began her examination. When finished, she looked at the imaging report. "You are fortunate this was found early. The mass is so small, I will need to insert a dye to find and remove it. We will talk about your treatment after the lumpectomy. Is that all right with you?"

Jamie sat up and sighed, able to breathe again. "Absolutely. How much time will I need to take off work for this?"

"Depending on what I find, the surgery will take less than two hours and you'll be in recovery another hour. This is usually an outpatient surgery, so you should not need to stay at the hospital overnight. For a couple of days, you may feel tired with some pain, but I can give you something for that if you wish. Then, you will be able to return to work."

"Thank you, Doctor."

"I know that you recently lost your husband. Do you have someone to help at home?"

"My sister is staying with me to help with my kids." Jamie smiled for the first time in a long while. "I have two kids, a teenage boy and a girl who's ten."

The doctor smiled and nodded. "I have two of my own. They are sweet, till they become teens. Well, we will schedule a follow-up appointment a few days after the surgery. Do you have any further questions?"

Jamie shook her head. "No, I appreciate your candor."

The surgery was scheduled and Jamie left the office.

CHAPTER 16

"WHAT THE HELL'S THAT?" Clyde Jamison yelled as he ran out of the barn on the Jamison Ranch. He was Nina's third son, who very seldom caused her any trouble, except for his brunette hair that hung down by his shoulders, which he knew his mother hated.

The sound of bulldozers shattering the usual peace on the ranch was coming from the direction of the old sawmill. Clyde ran back into the barn, where his saddled horse stood in the aisle.

"Come on, Whisper," he said as he mounted the Appaloosa that he'd been riding for over five years. The horse jolted forward and they raced out of the barn to find out who was responsible for the ruckus.

When he arrived at the early homestead, Clyde stopped his horse and jumped off. His brother, Jack, was standing with his hands on his hips, supervising the wrecking crew as they leveled the structure built in 1904 by Fergus, grandson of Callum Jamison. Taking a deep breath, Clyde tethered his horse next to Jack's bay-colored Quarter Horse and tried to calm his anger as he rushed up to his older sibling.

"Are you crazy?" Clyde yelled over the clamor. "Mom's going to kill you."

"She knows," Jack said, the hot sun making his red hair and beard look like he was on fire.

Clyde watched as the large machines made matchsticks out of something that he'd always been proud of. He and his eldest brother, Cal, would go up there when kids, pretending they were working the mill like their forefathers did decades before. Then, he saw numerous wooden posts marking certain areas around the property.

"What're those for?" he asked, pointing to the stakes.

"That's where I'm going to build cabins for our guests."

"What guests?"

"The vacationers who will come to stay on our ranch."

"You mean a dude ranch? Like out of the movie *City Slickers*?"

Jack laughed. "Something like that, but we won't let them move our cattle. They'll be here to relax and enjoy life in this pristine area of Oregon."

Clyde ran a hand through his dark hair that he'd inherited from his mother. His brother sounded like a TV advertisement he'd seen recently about a guest ranch in Washington doing the same thing.

"I've got to hand it to you," Clyde said, "You've got a big pair of balls. I'm not sure what Cal's going to have to say about this."

"He's not here," Jack said sharply.

Clyde knew Jack and Cal didn't get along, but many years ago he'd decided that was his job – to keep the peace in the family. Cal always seemed to have a chip on his shoulder and Clyde realized that now wasn't the time to bring it all up again.

Just then, their younger brother, Tate, galloped up on horseback in a cloud of dust. He jumped off and stood next to Clyde. "I was out on the south ridge when I saw these machines working. Jack, you're in real trouble now. Cal's not going to like this!"

"I don't give a damn what Cal thinks. This is my decision—"

Tate flew at Jack and Clyde quickly took a step back as the two men rolled to the ground in a brawl as fists connected with flesh, dust roiling around them.

"Awe, come on you two," Clyde said, trying to pull his brothers apart. "Cut it out!"

Before he knew it, Clyde was punched in the face and joined in on the fight. Arms and legs flew as the three young men clashed in the red dirt.

"STOP!" a woman's voice yelled from behind them.

Immediately, the men were being pulled apart by Wes, the ranch foreman. They all stood up, brushing dust from their clothes.

"You boys are too old for this kind of shit," Wes said.

Nina Jamison stared at her three sons as if they were still children.

"What is the meaning of this?" she asked, her arms crossed over her chest.

"Sorry, Mom," Jack and Tate said in unison.

"I was just trying to break them up when Jack hit me," Clyde said, wiping the blood from his mouth with the back of his hand.

"So, what brought this on?" she asked.

"Jack's tearing down the old sawmill," Clyde began, "and he's going to turn this place into a tourist attraction."

"What?!" Tate exclaimed.

"I know," Nina said. She looked at Wes and sighed. "It's best for the ranch."

Just then, a BMW drove up the long lane and parked near the log house.

"That's Mary Cresswell," Jack said, recognizing the car. He brushed the dirt off his shirt and pants. "I'll go see what she wants." He stopped and looked at his mother. "Can you take care of this mess?"

Nina smiled and said, "Wes and I have it under control."

Jack jumped onto his horse and rode off.

MARY STEPPED OUT OF her rental car. She looked around and saw a man on horseback riding toward her. He was the red-haired man she'd met earlier the last time she was on the ranch with Winnie. She remembered his broad shoulders and strong physique and wondered if he'd ever pose for her to paint him someday.

Jack dismounted and stood with the red-brown horse's reins in one hand.

"Hi," he said smiling. "You're Mary, Jamie's sister, right?"

"Yes," she said, "and you're Jack, Cal's brother." She held out her hand. "We weren't formally introduced the last time I was here."

Jack nodded and took her hand. "Nice to finally meet. Is there something I can help you with?"

"I was hoping to go near the river to look for more rocks for my paints. Winnie brought me last time."

Jack, still holding her hand, looked back toward the sawmill, and then said, "Well, it so happens I'm free. It might be easier if we go on horseback – do you ride?"

"I do," Mary said, smiling. "But it's been a while."

CHAPTER 17

OLIVIA JONES ARRIVED AT Riley Creswell's home. She was so glad when her dad gave her the Subaru Forester on her seventeenth birthday last summer, even if it was a used car. She knew Riley was jealous since he only had his dad's old pickup to drive.

She parked and went inside the house, carrying a white paper bag. She was a petite blonde like Riley's mom and she and Riley had been friends since Middle School. They'd only started dating their junior year.

"Anybody home?" she called out as she removed her red and white wool scarf and laid it on the counter, next to the broken trophy. She couldn't shake the look on Riley's face when he'd been nabbed by that mall security guard.

When no one answered, she took the bag out to the barn. Duke, the dog, followed the smell of what was in her bag. Riley was inside angrily mucking one stall, muttering under his breath.

"That asshole almost got me arrested and for what – a stupid trophy that I won as a kid?" he said to Champ, the horse tethered in the aisle. "And my mom grounded me on top of that!"

"Hey," Olivia said.

Riley quickly turned. "What're you doing here?"

"I brought lunch." She patted the white bag with the famous 'CHOW' logo.

"I hope you got burgers and fries," he said, smiling as he leaned the pitchfork against the stall.

"You'd better wash your hands, mister," she said.

As he walked to the small sink at one end of the barn, she asked, "I brought extra…isn't anyone else home?"

"No. Josie's at her friend's house, Mom's at work, and my aunt went to get some stupid rocks."

"What's Mary going to do with rocks?"

"I don't know – something to do with her painting. She's an artist, you know."

Olivia found a blanket to lay down on a bale of hay, sat down, and opened the bag. Duke hopefully sat down on the ground next to her feet. She wanted to ask Riley what he was going to do for New Year's Eve but thought now was not the time.

"Dang, that smells good," Riley said as he joined her. He looked at the sun coming through the open doors as it shimmered through her blonde hair. "Thanks."

"I was hoping you'd be in a better mood by now – after what happened at the mall." She took a French fry from the bag and ate it.

"I'm just so pissed." He took a large bite of the double cheeseburger.

"I know you're pissed about that, but is this maybe still about your dad?" she asked.

He looked up at her and chewed for a moment. After he swallowed and set his burger down, he wiped his mouth and hand with a napkin and sighed.

"You should be a therapist. You're good at this stuff

and can always see right through me."

Olivia put her arm on his shoulder and said, "I can always tell when something's bothering you."

"My mom won't talk to me about my dad - and I think there's something else going on."

"Why?"

"I don't know – it's just a feeling but I think my mom may be sick."

"Oh, I'm so sorry." Olivia hugged him.

They looked into each other's eyes. This was the closest they'd ever been before. Riley looked down at her soft lips and then back up into her cornflower-blue eyes. He leaned in slowly, to see how she would respond. When she moved toward him, he gently tasted the oil and salt from the French fry she'd eaten.

A moment later, they pulled apart. This was their first kiss and neither knew what to do next. Nervously he finally said, "My mom's going to be home soon. You'd probably better go."

Olivia, surprised at the quick change in Riley and a little hurt, got up and left.

CHAPTER 18

MARY AND JACK RODE along the same trail that Winnie had taken her before from the Jamison Ranch toward the Crooked River. Being on horseback gave Mary a new perspective on the area around her. Sagebrush littered the meadow where the tall Ponderosa pine stood. Then, as they guided their horses down the trail into the gorge, Mary looked up at the natural beauty of the majestic basalt canyon walls and rocky cliffs overhead. A bald eagle called out as it soared across the azure sky.

The chestnut mare named Dolly that Jack had chosen for her was gentle and easy to ride. She hadn't been on a horse since one summer a few years before when she came to visit her sister. Mary was glad she'd worn a down coat and heavy boots to protect herself from the chilly wind, and the sun felt good on her back.

"It is so beautiful here," she said as she quickly took pictures with her camera.

Jack nodded. "This is one of my favorite places. My brothers and I would come down here to swim in the river when it got hot in the summer. Where did you learn to ride?"

"Our family has a small farm by the town of Alfalfa, east of Bend." Mary laughed, then added, "Dad always called it a ranch, but it's only five acres and easy to manage. I was five when I first learned to ride on Mom's buckskin horse aptly named 'Buck.'"

They arrived down by the water's edge and she became excited as she dismounted. She took the small sample bag and tools she'd brought with her. "This is where Winnie brought me last time. I learned so much from her about which rocks make which pigment for paints."

"So, you're an artist," Jack said. He dismounted, took her horse's reins, and tethered the animals to a tree nearby.

"Yes, I work at a gallery in Seattle, but need to stay here a little longer to help Jamie – since Luther's gone."

"I understand and I'm sure she appreciates it. What type of medium do you use?"

Mary looked at Jack. "I generally like oils best, but Winnie was showing me some of her work in acrylics."

"I miss my grandmother," Jack sighed.

"You should go see her."

He shrugged and said, "It's complicated."

As they walked along the low-flowing winter river, Mary would stop and inspect some of the smaller rocks near the edge.

"Here's a yellow-looking agate," Jack said, pulling up a transparent stone. "Will this work?"

"Oh, yes," Mary said as she placed it in her bag. "And, I just found a beautiful opal. Winnie told me they were also found in these parts."

"I've walked along here thousands of times," Jack said, "but I had no idea rocks could be used for painting."

Mary smiled. "I'm also looking for some Jasper to make a red pigment."

"I think we've got that around here."

She picked up a reddish rock and started scraping it like Winnie had shown her to reveal the true sedimentary color beneath the surface.

Mary said, excitedly, "I can make a burnt umber color with this if I mix in some yellow and red with a blue base paint."

"You sure do get enthusiastic about your art," Jack said.

"I started as a little girl fingerpainting. It's my true passion." She looked at Jack and added, "I think it's important to follow your heart."

Jack smiled and nodded. "Maybe sometime I could take you to one of the Sunstone mines south of here. Sunstone is Oregon's official gem and it comes in all colors."

"Oh, I would love that!"

THEY CONTINUED SEARCHING FOR rocks for some time, then Mary said she had enough samples for now and put her tools away.

They mounted their horses and Jack took a different route back toward the ranch house. The trail led to where the excavation had taken place. The bulldozers stood idle now next to a large pile of logs.

Eventually, he stopped at a place near the river where some wooden stakes marked certain areas across the meadow.

"What are those markers for?" she asked.

"We're thinking of converting an area of the ranch for guests to stay, sort of like a retreat. Those indicate where each future cabin will be."

"I like the idea and would gladly come to stay here when you're finished. You could also do weddings and other big events."

"Absolutely," Jack said excitedly. "I've even thought about corporate packages."

Mary smiled. "Maybe you found your passion. You know, advertising this through a website is a great idea. Social media today is a big advantage for marketing. I worked on our gallery's site." As she looked over the area, ideas swirled in her head. "I wish I could help, but I'll be leaving for Seattle in a few days."

Jack looked at her and said, "I wish you didn't have to go back north."

She sighed. "Me, too."

Mary realized how ruggedly handsome the man next to her was. He was taller than her and his black Stetson hat shaded his face, but she could see that his blue shirt matched his eyes.

As they walked farther around the area, Jack showed her where the larger event center and each cabin would be. She was impressed with his vision and could see through his words what the place would eventually look like.

When they came to where the horses stood, he turned to her and said, "There's something I have to ask. Are you and my brother, Cal, together?"

She looked at him in surprise. "We've only been on a couple of dates...but I think we're better just being friends."

Jack smiled. "Well then, would you like to join us for dinner tonight? I'm sure Ma won't mind and she'd like to get to know you."

Mary thought for a moment and said, "I'll have to call Jamie and let her know." She looked at her watch and added, "She should be getting home about now."

CHAPTER 19

JAMIE PARKED HER CAR at Creswell Ranch with Josie, who was a little disheveled, which was so unlike her. Every morning before school, the little princess took forever to get ready.

"How was your time at Susie's?" Jamie asked to quiet the voices in her head from her doctor's appointment.

"It was okay," her daughter sighed and tugged at her jacket. "Her mom made some vegetarian thingy for lunch and made us go outside and play in the snow. That was fun, but then you came and I didn't have enough time to get my stuff organized."

"You never have enough time, but you always look nice."

"You're my mom. You're supposed to say things like that." Excitedly, Josie turned in her seat and said, "Susie and I were making plans for my birthday party."

"That's not until next May," Jamie said, thankful for the switch in the conversation.

"But, it's never too early to start!"

WHEN THEY WALKED INTO the kitchen, Jamie found a voice message from Mary that she was having dinner at the Jamisons. At first, she was angry that Mary had not been there for Riley, since she'd grounded him, but was hoping to have a few moments to herself.

Riley came out of the living room. "Hey, squirt," he said to his sister.

"Cowboy," she answered, using her favorite nickname for him.

Together, he and Josie both asked their mother, "What's for dinner?"

Jamie looked around in a daze, then opened the refrigerator. She stood there for a few moments, not really seeing anything appetizing in front of her.

"Well?" Riley asked.

She knew it was too far for delivery to their place, and she didn't want to drive back into town. Jamie opened the freezer, turned, and asked, "How about frozen pizza?"

"We had that last night," Josie whined. "Where's Aunt Mary? We like her cooking."

"She's not coming home for dinner tonight," Jamie snapped. "Go to your rooms. I'll let you know when it's ready."

Both kids stomped up the stairs and each slammed their bedroom doors.

After Jamie put the pizza in the oven, she went into the living room and opened a hutch where Luther kept his bottle of Jack Daniels. It wasn't her alcohol of choice, but it was all she had in the house at the moment. She took out a glass, poured a stiff drink, and quickly drank it. She winced at the taste, but poured another glass and sank down onto the couch. *CANCER!* The word kept circling in her head. Scared and alone, she now became disappointed that she couldn't share her news with her sister and figure out what she was going to do next.

When the timer went off in the kitchen, she walked back in. That's when she saw Olivia's scarf lying on the counter. She knew it was Riley's girlfriend's because she'd bought it for Riley at a local shop that sold alpaca wool clothes to give to her on one of her birthdays.

Her son came in and saw his mother holding the scarf.

"What is this doing here?" Jamie asked.

"Olivia brought me lunch. She must've forgotten it."

"Was Aunt Mary here then?"

Riley gazed down at the kitchen tile and said, "No." Then he quickly looked up at his mom and said, "But, Olivia didn't stay long."

He frowned as he watched his mother quietly set the scarf back on the counter, take the pizza out, and put it on the stovetop. He'd expected a lecture again about the birds and the bees. But, without saying another word, she only pulled two plates from the cabinet and went back into the living room without taking any food. He'd seen the alcohol on the coffee table and sighed heavily. This was what his dad always did when something was bothering him. Now, Riley really was scared.

CHAPTER 20

WHEN MARY RETURNED, SHE was surprised a cold, half-eaten pizza was still sitting on the counter, which was so unlike her well-organized sister. Then, she found Jamie sitting alone in the living room, holding a red and white scarf in her lap.

"Hi, hon," she said as she sat in an armchair next to the couch. "I had a wonderful time getting to know the Jamison family today. Jack is an interesting guy—" Mary stopped when she saw the bottle and glass next to her sister, which she knew Jamie never did.

Mary went to the couch and sat down next to her sister. "What's wrong," she asked. "Are you ok?"

"No, dammit," Jamie yelled. "Everything is not okay. You were supposed to be here with Riley."

"I did call and thought you would be home soon—"

"Olivia came by while no one else was here. Those two kids were alone, unsupervised." Jamie showed her the scarf. "This is Olivia's – it was in the kitchen when I got home."

"I'm sure nothing happened with them," Mary said. "They're good kids—" She stopped when Jamie began to cry. She put her arm around her older sister. "What's wrong, Sis?"

Between sobs, Jamie tried to tell her about the doctor's appointment and prognosis.

"My surgery date is next month. Happy New Year!"

"So soon?" Mary asked as she picked up a Kleenex box from the table and handed one to her sister.

Jamie nodded and blew her nose. "Yeah, that scared me, too."

Mary tucked Jamie's hair behind one ear and said, "I'm sure everything will be all right."

"You don't know…" Jamie began to cry again.

Jamie usually was the strongest one in the family. Not sure what else to say, Mary tried to assure her sister. "I'm here now and I'll stay as long as you need me. I'll call the Seattle gallery and explain everything. I'm sure they'll understand."

Neither woman knew that Riley was standing in the stairwell and heard everything.

CHAPTER 21

THE MAN, STILL WEARING his disguise, was sitting in a booth in the D&D Bar and Grill in downtown Bend. Earlier, at the Redmond airport, he'd waited for Ramirez's plane to arrive and followed the younger man to the car rental desk. When he overheard him ask for the location of the D&D, he knew where this place was located. So, he'd taken the gray SUV parked at the airport freight terminal and driven here in order to arrive before Ramirez.

Colored lights were lit in the overhang above the bar and the bartender turned on two TV screens. It was early and there were few people there. The smell of frying bacon, coffee, and hot grease filled the room. Four young men sat near the front window wearing ski outfits. *It's been a long time since I was on Mt. Bachelor*, the man thought.

He smiled when his target entered the building and sat at the bar. The bartender came over, placed a small napkin down, and asked, "What'll you have?"

Ramirez looked at his watch. "A Bloody Mary."

The bartender went to work on the drink just as a young Asian woman came in from the back of the building.

"Well, Larry Johnson," she said to the bartender as she put on an apron. "Why isn't Barney opening today?"

"He's sick with the flu," Larry said. "I'm only here temporarily until he gets to feeling better."

A bell rang, signaling an order was ready in the kitchen.

"Would you take this to that old guy over there, Hana?" Larry asked as he handed her the plate of pancakes.

"Sure," Hana said as she grabbed a coffee pot.

The man didn't smile at the woman as she set the plate before him. He just watched as the bartender set the Bloody Mary in front of Ramirez.

"Can I get you anything else, sir?" the waitress asked, filling his coffee mug.

"No," he said gruffly.

After she left, he heard Ramirez ask the bartender, "What time do you think Cal Jamison will come in? I know he comes here almost every day for breakfast."

"I heard Cal is gone."

"When will he be back?"

"Don't know – maybe a week, maybe more."

The man became angry – not finding Jamison was a delay in his mission.

Then Ramirez said, "I saw a brochure at the airport for Paulina Lake. I'd recognized it since Cal talked about it before – when we were together. Can you tell me how to get there?"

The man smiled and finished his pancakes. He knew where Paulina Lake was.

CHAPTER 22

THE TOTAL FLIGHT TIME from North Carolina to Red Cloud, Nebraska was over fifteen hours, requiring an overnight stop at Olney-Noble Field in Illinois. On his flight, Cal was angry that his CO had waited until he'd been released from active duty to tell him about new intel on the blast he a year ago, but he also understood. A vendetta – revenge was never the answer. It wouldn't bring his men back… By the time he landed, he was much calmer.

A guy at the Municipal Airport knew Angel and gave Cal a ride to his friend's trailer, but Angel was not at home. So, the man dropped him off at the Palace Steakhouse Lounge where he said the locals usually go to eat.

Cal sat at the bar and ordered a Char-Burger, onion rings, and a beer. He looked at the black wall next to him and saw hundreds of signatures in white ink of men and women in all branches of the military and the years they'd served. He leaned in closer and saw Angel's name and rank.

"Impressive, isn't it?" a silver-haired man next to him asked.

Cal nodded. "Can anybody sign it? Do you have to be

from here?"

"No, just military."

"I'm a Marine," Cal said, not yet ready to admit he was on terminal leave.

The man handed him a white pen and Cal signed his name as close to Angel's as he could.

"I know this man," Cal said, pointing to his friend's signature.

"Me, too." The man reached out his hand and said, "I'm Ken Whitaker. Angel works for me."

"I came here to see him, but he wasn't home. We were in the Marines together. Do you know where I can find him?"

Ken shook his head. "Not really, he just left a few days ago. Didn't say where he was going or when he'd be back. He'd do that sometimes. He might've gone toward Haigler to be near the mountains again – the same place some old man that just came through here was headed. We don't get many strangers in these parts, but there was something about that guy that I couldn't put my finger on…"

"I appreciate you telling me," Cal said.

The silver-haired man took a sip of his beer and added, "I know more than Angel lets on. He never talks about how he lost his leg, but I've been in battle before, too. I was in the Gulf War in '91 during Operation Desert Storm. I flew UH-60A Black Hawk helicopters doing combat rescue. While I was there, I met a fine lady who worked on our choppers – but I lost track of her…"

CHAPTER 23

ANGEL ARRIVED AT THE Paulina Lake Lodge on a snowmobile he'd rented from a guy at the Ten Mile Sno-Park since the road to the lodge was closed because of the recent snowstorm. As he got off the machine, his leg ached from the cold.

He looked up at the large log building with snowdrifts around its base. Trails had been cleared and a red sleigh sat out in the snow nearby. Smiling, he wondered if they used large elk or Santa's reindeer to pull the sleigh at Christmas time.

He saw a group of three pretty women walk into the lodge's restaurant. One smiled at him, a lovely brunette with striking blue eyes. Angel followed them. Behind the registration desk stood an older hippie with a braided, long, red beard and bright purple, Peruvian-style ski hat with ear flaps.

"My name is Bud Smithe with an 'e' – how can I help?" the clerk said.

Angel brushed snow from his jacket and smiled. "I don't have a reservation, but wondered if you have a room for one for a week?"

"We just had a cancellation for a small cabin."

"Perfect. I'll take it."

Bud had the newcomer sign in and handed him a key. "Follow the trail to the right of the lodge and you'll find your cabin. We have Happy Hour in the Cocktail Bar, and tonight's the Saturday Prime Rib and Cobbler dinner."

"Do I need a reservation?"

"It wouldn't hurt. People come here from all over for that."

Angel made the dinner reservation, picked up some trail maps of the area, and then walked out. The lake was pristine in the crisp December air, with a long dock leading out toward the thin icy water. Footprints led down the dock and stopped at the empty boat ramps. The footprints reminded him that Bud had told him that cellphones only worked if you walked out onto the dock.

The sun was setting behind the trees as he rode his snowmobile to the cabin. The small red-metal roof was mostly covered in snow. As he removed his bag from the machine, two deer scampered through the evergreens. One stopped and looked at him, then followed the other along a trail near the lake. It reminded Angel of his childhood home.

THE CABIN WAS RUSTIC inside with one large room containing a couple of brown plaid-covered chairs and a couch that probably was a hide-a-bed. A small kitchen stood on the left and he was thankful to see a small private bathroom with a shower. The inside of the walls were varnished logs, caulk filled the gaps to help insulate the place. As he hung his coat on a peg by the door, he remembered that Bud had also told him there was no TV,

Wi-Fi, or radio reception in the cabins. Angel hadn't been 'unplugged' from the world for some time and it felt very calming.

In the narrow bedroom, which had a double-sized bed, he unpacked a few items from his bag. Angel checked the inside pocket of his fleece vest where he'd placed the coded message he'd written for Cal, a reminder of why he was in Oregon. Then he put the garment at the bottom of his bag under other clothes before leaving the bedroom.

He looked at his cellphone. He saw all the past missed calls from Cal and was filled with guilt. They had been together for years in the Marines, but now he was blowing off his best friend because he couldn't cope with his lot in life.

He sat in one of the chairs by the couch for about a half hour. It was too quiet now and getting colder. Using the offline mode on his phone, he found some audio files he'd downloaded and started a song by Reba McEntire about being a survivor.

Angel took a cigarette out of his pocket, then frowned when he saw the 'No Smoking' sign by the door. Putting the cigarette behind one ear, he was pleased to see a wood stove off to one side of the large room. He'd seen some chopped wood under the small porch outside. So, he went out and grabbed some, then started a fire and sat down again to read the brochures. He noticed the lodge was built in 1929, and the Newbery Volcano, which shaped the area thousands of years ago, was still active. A snowmobile trail map looked interesting, with possible access to a hot spring, waterfalls, and Paulina Peak.

Angel went to the kitchen, filled his gray thermos with tap water at the sink, and set it next to his box of meds – like he did every night. A new song began which he knew – *Colder Weather* by the Zac Brown Band. As he listened to the lyrics, a face came to mind of Heather, his high school girlfriend. She'd written to him all those years while he was in the service, and when he came home after his last tour, he was going to propose to her. He'd even bought a ring at one of the airport duty shops. However, once she saw what had happened to him, she couldn't handle his disabilities and broke up with him. That's when he tossed the ring into a lake outside his home and moved to Nebraska.

He looked at his watch and saw he had a little time before dinner and decided he needed a drink.

THE MAN OUTSIDE HAD been following Ramirez and was watching through a small window on a side of the remote cabin that backed up to the forest. He couldn't believe his luck at how easy this all was so far.

He saw one of his target's habits with the thermos and medicine box near the sink and realized what he needed to do.

After Ramirez left the cabin, the man checked the door of the cabin and was relieved it was unlocked. *People are so naïve in these areas, thinking they are safe*, he thought smiling as he quickly entered. Once inside, he went to the kitchen area and pulled a small mouthwash bottle out of the inside pocket of his coat. Then, he poured the contents into the thermos.

CHAPTER 24

BECAUSE CAL HAD SEEN the weather report before leaving Red Cloud, he'd decided he needed to stay overnight. Taking advantage of the weather, he flew the short distance and landed his plane at the Millard Municipal Airport, a few miles from downtown Omaha, and called for an Uber. There was something he wanted to investigate while he was in Nebraska.

The Magnolia Hotel was a gorgeous structure with a bar and a courtyard in the center. It was built in 1923, and beautifully designed after a palace in Florence, Italy. As he was checking in, he knew he was on a mission of his own. But after he did a bit of work before it got dark, he was looking forward to a great dinner in the hotel's restaurant and a quiet evening alone.

It was almost New Year's Eve and he was missing his family, but somehow, he knew he needed to do this. He wasn't sure why, but he was hoping to find closure for Jordan. He understood what it was like to lose a parent without knowing who caused it or why it had to happen. He still didn't know who shot his dad when he was out mending fences alone on one of the ranges at the Jamison Ranch when Cal was only sixteen. He never got over that.

The downtown branch of the Omaha Library was only a two-minute walk from the hotel. A plaque near the historic building entrance noted that the city of Omaha was established in 1854, but he knew there were early Native American tribes in the area long before that. Somewhere he'd read that as early as 1804, Lewis and Clark stopped at Fort Calhoun and met with people of the Oto and Missouri Tribes. This made him think of his Northern Paiute grandmother and her family's history.

Wyanet, also known as 'Winnie' as she liked to be called, was born and raised on the Warm Springs Reservation near Culver, Oregon. At nineteen, she met Glenn Jamison when he came into the bakery in Bend where she was working. She knew the history of her people but did not live through most of the tragedy of her tribe. Cal remembered her telling how her grandfather sometimes got so angry that her mother had to calm him down. He now thought of one time when Winnie told him, 'I am thankful for my life now, but I will never forget my family's past.'

As Cal walked through the library, he smiled as he remembered the first time he met Jordan Hansen, the medical examiner in Bend. It was last fall, during Luther's murder investigation. She had ridden up to the crime scene on a motorcycle with her cadaver dog riding shotgun in the sidecar.

During the investigation, Jordan mentioned that her parents were killed in Omaha during a home invasion that was never solved. He'd decided on the flight east that if he was going to see Angel in Nebraska, he wanted to find out more about that case. If he was going to be a private investigator in his civilian life, he might as well start somewhere.

Cal went down to the archive section of the library to search through the microfilm database for possible newspaper articles about Jordan and her family. He thought of calling Micco for some help, but since he hadn't told his friend yet about this little side trip, he decided against it. His experience in the military was all the help he needed on this job.

The first search on Jordan's name brought up an article about her medical school graduation. The article mentioned her mother, Grace Hansen. He sat back when a photo of a young Jordan came up on the screen. She was beautiful and her eyes were filled with excitement and wonder. He looked around the empty room, then took a picture of the screen with his phone camera. He remembered she'd mentioned that she'd been the one to find her parents murdered in their home. Another search showed Jordan's residency was at the Omaha University Medical Center.

He could find no reference to a murder case with her mother's name, but there was another case about the same time Jordan graduated on an Edwin Wilcox and his wife. Photos of the incident were horrific and he was surprised the paper had been allowed to print them. He noticed that the crime scene looked like the room had been ransacked as if the killer was searching for something, but he'd have to see if there was any way either he or Micco could get a copy of the police report if this murder was connected.

There were images of the two victims. Cal stared at the dead woman's face. She was the spitting image of Jordan. He also took closeup photos of these pictures and then printed the articles.

One of the items mentioned that Wilcox had been a professor at the university. Cal did a Google Map search and found that the campus was too far to walk today, so he decided to wait and see what he could learn there the next day.

As he left the library and walked to the hotel, he rolled his shoulders and realized how exhausted he was. He really hadn't taken any time to recover from the long flight to North Carolina and the emotional roller-coaster ride of leaving his life's career behind. But then, remembering some of the long tours he'd had to endure in the Marines, he took a deep breath and marched on. He wished he could've seen Angel and wondered where his friend would've gone…

CHAPTER 25

ANGEL SAT ON A stool in the cocktail bar next to the Lake Paulina Lodge restaurant. The smells coming from the kitchen were heavenly. He ordered a Maker's Mark Bourbon on the rocks and looked around the rustic room. The fire in the large stone hearth warmed the open area. Along a few of the log walls hung various mounted fish that he was certain probably came with great fishing stories he'd read about.

He thought of Cal and the stories he used to tell when they were on duty overseas. It was Cal's way of bringing a bit of home to his team, getting them to think about times they'd been with family and friends instead of whatever wasteland they were stationed at.

A group of women sat at the other end of the bar wearing colorful wool sweaters and jeans, one was the brunette he'd seen when he'd checked into the lodge. The young woman's eyes met his. She smiled, walked over with her drink, and sat next to him.

"Hi, I'm Leslie," she said as she offered her hand.

"Angel," he said as their fingers touched.

"Do you come here often, Angel?"

"This is my first time. How about you?"

"I'm just visiting the area with my friends. We went skiing on Mt. Bachelor today. After we checked in here, we heard about the amazing Saturday night dinners."

"I'm waiting for a friend."

She got up to leave. "I'm sorry—"

He placed his hand on her arm and said, "No, I meant I'm killing time up here until my friend returns to Bend. I skied Mt. Hood once – a long time ago."

She smiled and sat down again.

Angel watched as an older man came in alone and took a seat at a table not far from where they were sitting.

"Are you from around here?" she asked.

"No…I live in Nebraska now." He noticed that her glass was almost empty. "Can I get you another drink?"

"Sure."

He motioned to the bartender and Leslie ordered a Grey Goose Vodka neat. He ordered another drink for himself.

"So," he said after the bartender left, "you're a skier."

"Yes. I'm from Utah and I've skied Alta since I was a kid. The snow there is a dry powder, not like the wet snow here."

"I grew up in a town west of Denver, Colorado. I've skied a lot of places, but my favorite was heli-skiing the Black Diamond Trails in Vail."

"That's available at the Snowbird Resort near Alta, but I've never done that."

Their drinks arrived.

"A few years ago, I took a train with some friends to Whitefish, Montana," Leslie said. "It was the first weekend in December when the ski resort opened. The snow there was beautiful, a lot like Alta." She brushed a long strand of hair behind her ear and added, "We practically took over an entire train car and partied all the way there. The train stopped in Spokane to hook up with another one from Seattle that had the dining and sleeper cars before continuing to Chicago. While we waited for the connection process, there was time to run to a nearby bar for a drink." She laughed and said, "If there was snow in Spokane, we knew the snow on the mountain would be good. The town of Whitefish was all decorated for Christmas. It was heavenly."

"Sounds like a great trip. I haven't been to Alta, what's it like?"

"It's a lovely ski town in the Wasatch Mountains and my favorite place of all, but then, it's also home. Most of my family still live there. When the sun is out, the skiing is pure joy. But, on cloudy days, it can be treacherous when there are shadows in the canyons."

Angel was going to say he'd have to check it out, until he realized that for the first time in over a year, he'd forgotten he no longer skied – not with his artificial leg. He took a sip of his drink instead.

"What's Nebraska like?" she asked.

He said, "Different…have you been to the Hot Springs here?"

"No."

"I'm going up there tomorrow on my snowmobile. Want to ride along?"

"That sounds great."

Just then, Leslie's friends came over to take her to the dining room. She introduced them to Angel and then asked him if he wanted to join them.

He looked at the other women. "Do you mind?"

"Absolutely not," the others said in unison.

After they left the bar, the old man remained and

ordered another drink, knowing that he had plenty of time to wait..

CHAPTER 26

IN OMAHA, CAL STEPPED out of the Uber car and pulled his flight jacket collar up around his ears as he walked through the university campus to find a directory. Some snowflakes were starting to swirl around in the cold wind. He was hoping to locate someone he could talk with to get some answers to the questions he'd uncovered at the library the day before.

He would've liked to enjoy sleeping in a bit today to get some well-deserved rest but wanted to leave Omaha soon to head home. It was about a six-hour flight to Oregon. He pulled his cap down tighter over his head.

One of the articles he'd found at the library mentioned that Dr. Wilcox had been a professor in the technical field at the university many years ago. Somewhere he'd read the entire campus covered hundreds of acres. He'd seen which building the Computer Science Department was in and headed that way, not sure what he was going to find. As he neared the Peter Kiewit Institute, he wasn't surprised to see there were very few people around since it was a holiday weekend. Then, he thought of how Jordan had probably walked this same area years before when she was getting her undergraduate degree.

Outside the large building, a tall, thin man with wheat-colored hair walked up to Cal and offered his hand. "Hi, my name is Kurt Stone. You look sort of lost. Can I help you find where you want to go?"

Cal noted that this man was about his age and had a strong handshake.

"My name is Cal Jamison and I'm looking for information about Dr. Edwin Wilcox."

Kurt took a step back. "Good lord, he's been dead for ten years."

"I know," Cal said. "I'm a friend of Jordan Hansen—"

"Well, there's another name from the past I haven't heard in a long time," Kurt said. "Jordan and I went to Med school and residency here together."

Cal looked around and asked, "Is there somewhere we can talk?"

"Sure, there's a small java shop across the street. Come with me and I'll buy you a coffee."

THERE WERE ONLY A few young people in the place. "Some of the students stick around even during the holidays," Kurt said as he ordered their coffee.

"So, if you're a doctor, why are you still on campus and not working in some hospital?" Cal asked.

"I'm a professor now at the university's Medical Center. During Med school, I was studying surgery and learned that I'm better at academics than in the OR – I couldn't handle the hours. I was over here today talking with a former student who is also considering switching fields, like I did."

Kurt paid for their drinks and they sat at a small table

near a bank of windows. After they were settled, a slender man with graying hair sat at a table near them and began reading a newspaper.

"How do you know Jordan?" Kurt asked as he put sugar in his coffee.

Cautiously, Cal said, "We met in San Diego."

"What line of work are you in?"

"I'm in the Marines," he said, even though he recently retired from the military.

Cal pulled the copies of the newspaper articles from his jacket and laid them on the table. "I wanted to find something about Jordan's parents but found nothing on the name Hansen. Is this Wilcox family somehow connected to her?"

Kurt nodded. "I'm afraid so. They were killed while a group of us were in Hawaii after we finished our residency. Jordan found them when we returned."

"It must have been horrible for her to see her parents like that…"

"Traumatizing. She was never the same after that." Kurt paused, then added, "I still wish I'd made more of an effort to stay in touch, but she left Omaha soon after their funeral without saying where she was going."

Cal, thinking of Angel, said, "I know what you mean… May I ask why the different surnames?"

"Wilcox was Jordan's stepfather. He never adopted her and she was given her mother's name, Hansen, when she was born. I don't think she knows anything about her biological father."

"How long was Wilcox working here?"

"I think his job was the reason they moved here from the east coast about thirty years ago. Dr. Wilcox was a brilliant professor. But then, just before he and his wife were murdered, he had quit his job here at the university and no one seemed to know why."

Cal's instinct from his military experience made him a bit suspicious about this news.

"I think Jordan still owns that house," Kurt added, then started talking about the time their alumni group had spent in Hawaii.

"We started on Oahu, then traveled by small plane to Moloka'i before flying home from Maui." Kurt laughed. "I remember us all riding donkeys down the steep slopes to the Leper colony. That night, we sat outside our condo drinking champagne while looking out over the Kalohi Channel, watching the one stoplight on the east side of Maui change. We laughed because the island we were on had no stoplights at all. It was a fabulous trip."

Cal checked his watch and said, "I've taken up enough of your time. Thank you, Kurt, for your help."

"Be careful out there – there's a storm coming. Happy New Year!"

BEFORE RETURNING TO THE hotel, Cal asked his Uber driver to take him to Jordan's parents' house. The address was on one of the articles.

He walked around the outside of the 1911 Bungalow-style, two-story, brown and tan home that had a wrap-around porch and large glass window in the front. Cal could see furniture still inside and wondered if anyone lived there now. The backyard was fenced, enclosing two old apple trees; and the long driveway down the left side led to a large three-car garage with stairs on one side leading up to what looked like an apartment above.

The place looked like it was well preserved and the landscaping was nicely groomed, but there was no evidence of life inside.

CHAPTER 27

IT WAS LATE WHEN Cal was in his hotel room in downtown Omaha. The weather on the TV channel was constantly showing images of the storm that had now accumulated, grounding Cal for another day. He turned it off and called his grandparents to let them know where he was.

"Cal, boy, how're you doin'?" Glenn's voice bellowed.

Cal smiled as he said, "I'm well…how are you two? I miss you."

"We are great! You're grandmother's here, too."

"Hi, sweetie," Winnie said. "Where are you now?"

"I'm in Omaha, Nebraska," Cal said, then quickly added, "I'll be heading home tomorrow, if weather permits. How's everything there with you all?"

The old man talked about how well the cattle and horses were doing after the storm passed them. Winnie said she was looking forward to hugging him again.

After he hung up, Cal looked over a flight plan he'd made for his return to Oregon after this storm lifted. He called Micco to let him know his approximate ETA. Then, he thought of Angel and wondered where he would've gone this time of year. He knew his friend no longer skied, but the man still loved his snow and mountains - at least, the man Cal knew before he'd disappeared.

Cal swore to himself that he hadn't made more of an effort to contact Angel before now and began to worry he may have lost his friend, as well as the other men in his unit. He went to the mini-bar and pulled out a small bottle of whiskey. As he poured the liquid into a glass, he wished he'd thought to buy some Glenfiddich before returning to his hotel.

He looked around his room and went to the desk where he had all the papers spread out that he'd found about Jordan and her family. One article said it was a home robbery, but the article didn't give any detail about anything that was stolen. In fact, the information given by the police was pretty sketchy, at best. He made notes of his discussion with Kurt and about his own suspicions.

Then, he turned the TV back on and found a country music channel. Surfing through the titles, he found a song by Alan Jackson called *Remember When*. This made him think of Sarah Leisner. Cal walked over to where his wallet lay on the table near the bed. He pulled out the photo he'd found when he was at Camp Lejeune. Sarah's beautiful face and smile stared back at him.

She was a funny girl. She loved to talk about her hometown - Fredericksburg, Virginia, where the city changed hands between the North and the South many times during the Civil War. The history was fascinating and Cal loved to sit for hours letting her drone on with her lovely accent about the stories of her family there. Sarah was dead now and he knew he needed to let her go, but he wasn't ready yet. He put the photo back into his wallet.

Cal sat down in a chair facing the wide window where

the lights of the city gleamed and sipped his whiskey. He leaned back as a different song came on with Billy Currington, singing about a woman needing directions. He could visualize the images of a guy in a cowboy hat helping a lady find her way but hoped she'd stay with him. Thoughts of the other women he'd recently met flooded through his mind.

He and Mary Cresswell had only been out a few times, but he found it hard to want to take it any further than just the occasional coffee or dinner. She was going to be leaving for Seattle soon, anyway. So, he thought of where this was going and decided that when he got back home, he needed to tell her that he hoped they could remain friends.

And then there was Jordan. She was a mystery that got under his skin, even though she had some of the same interests as him in aviation and solving puzzles. Jordan was beautiful and highly intelligent, but she also seemed to keep a distance between them. Like him, she had her secrets. He wasn't sure if he was going to tell her what he'd just done – looking into her parents' murders. He felt he didn't really know her well enough yet.

SUDDENLY, A LARGE BANG shook his hotel room window and then a burst of light followed. Cal immediately fell to the floor - he was back in Afghanistan with the sounds and images of the attack flying through his mind. His heart was racing and his body was in pain from the shrapnel of the IED that ripped through his flesh. It took quite a few moments before he finally realized that he wasn't bleeding – he was in Omaha, not Sangin and the holiday fireworks outside had started.

He got up from the floor and his hand shook as he emptied the whiskey in his glass. These flashbacks were rare these days, but there usually was some trigger that caused them – like sounds that reminded him of explosions. During his recovery, even before he'd returned to Oregon, he'd worked with a therapist for months at the veteran's hospital. Re-living that event by talking through it was the saving grace that helped him to learn what he needed to avoid and how to deal with his memories. He still had not worked through his own guilt that maybe he could have done something differently to save his men. His therapist told him that would take time.

Looking out his window, he tried to relax as he watched the shapes and colors burst in the night sky. A new year usually felt like a reason to resolve to make changes, but this time, he was unsure which direction he'd be taking. When the array was finished, he went to the mini-bar and got out another bottle and wondered if he would ever find true love again…or forgive himself.

CHAPTER 28

ANGEL AND LESLIE HAD been out all day and it was getting late after the New Year's Eve dinner party at the lodge when they arrived at his cabin. The fire was out in the stove and it was chilly inside.

"This place is so tiny, it won't take long to heat up," Angel said as he built a new fire and lit it.

Leslie sat on the couch, which was more the size of a loveseat, and left her coat on until heat permeated from the stove. "What a fun day. I can't believe how wonderful and diverse this place is. The hot springs were amazing and I didn't expect the tall twin falls to be frozen so early."

He stood up and said, "We're at an altitude of over six thousand feet and it is January. Maybe tomorrow I could take you up to Paulina Peak on my snowmobile. I hear the view can be awesome if this weather holds. On a clear day, from there you can see Mt. Shasta in northern California, all the way up to Washington's Mt. Adams."

"I'd love that!"

The room began to warm. "Our cabin is much larger than this one," Leslie said as she looked around and removed her coat. "But there are three women in ours."

"I like this one," he said. "It reminds me of home."

Angel hung her coat on a peg by the door. He was nervous. He hadn't been with a woman since Afghanistan – because of his leg. To stall for time, he took off his own jacket and opened a new bottle of Maker's Mark he always packed when traveling.

"I don't have any vodka," he said, then showed her the label. "Will this work to help warm you up?"

"Sure," Leslie said. "I know you're probably talking about Colorado since the only skiing I know of in Nebraska is on Mount Crescent."

"Yeah, it's more of a ski hill than a mountain, but I don't ski anymore."

"So, what's wrong with your leg?" she finally asked.

He stopped and looked at her.

"I noticed you were limping earlier but didn't say anything. It must've been hard to ride that snowmobile so long today."

Angel went to her and handed her a glass of golden liquid. "It usually does about this time of day," he said and sat next to her.

During drinks, he told her a short version of what had happened to him. "Some guys in the military get injured like this and go back in…but my head was too messed up. Besides PTSD, I sometimes have depression and…I forget things. I moved from my hometown to disappear in Nebraska."

"You probably also suffered a TBI – traumatic brain injury."

"How do you know all this?"

"I received an Occupational Therapy Doctorate at Pacific University. I'm now doing a course on Amputee Rehabilitation. That's what brought me to Oregon." Then she asked softly, "Would you permit me to see your prosthetic device?"

Other than the doctors and therapists at the VA hospitals, he'd never allowed anyone to see his stump. After a long moment, Angel nodded.

Leslie went down on one knee and pushed up his right pant leg, then carefully took off the socket and sleeve. His residual limb was swollen and red from the abrasion of the prosthetic. She noticed that it was an older rigid model socket.

"It gets like this if I use it too much," he said.

"Let me help with this."

She went to the kitchen, found some clean towels, and filled a bowl with warm soapy water. Sitting down on the floor, she gently cleansed the skin. "My dad was in the Army and had a prosthetic arm. That's why I got into the field."

Leslie examined the device and added, "You may just have the wrong type of socket. Technology has advanced so much for suspension prostheses."

Angel relaxed back onto the couch and sighed. "You're the first person to understand what I'm really going through."

As she dried the limb and reapplied the device. Then, she sat next to him again and said, "If you want, I could contact the Portland VA Medical Center – they have specialty care services that could maybe help you."

Finally, Angel was filled with hope. He then decided to maybe try a new device and make changes to get better. Maybe someday he'd even ski again. He reached out a hand and touched her hair. Then, he leaned in and softly kissed her. Her lips tasted a bit like strawberries from the dessert she'd had at dinner.

"I don't know how to thank you," he said.

She smiled at him. “I do…”
Leslie took his hand and led him to the bedroom.

CHAPTER 29

THAT NIGHT, THE MAN had seen Ramirez and the brunette in the lodge at dinner. He followed them to Angel's cabin and patiently waited in the trees outside for the woman to leave.

Finally, the door opened and he heard her say, "I'll meet you for breakfast tomorrow, then maybe we can go up to the Peak." She kissed Ramirez and then walked away.

The man looked in the small window and smiled as his victim went to the kitchen and took his medicine, drinking from the thermos. He saw Ramirez wince and hoped he'd blame the bitter taste on the local water, not the poison he'd placed there earlier. Then, he looked at his watch and waited. He knew it could take a while before the poison took effect, but he always liked to take his time on a job – like a cat playing with a mouse.

LATER, AS THE MAN opened the door with his gloved hand, he heard Ramirez say, "Did you forget something, Leslie?"

Ramirez looked at the older man and said, "Are you lost, sir?" Then, he put his hand to his stomach as he became nauseous, ran to the kitchen sink and vomited. "What the hell?" Ramirez exclaimed.

Smiling, the man stepped inside and closed the door. As he watched his victim exhibit other expected symptoms of the poison he'd given him, he closed the curtain over the small window.

"Remember me?" the older man asked.

Fear grabbed Angel – he knew that voice! He tried to attack the man as best he could, but the only thing he accomplished was to pull at the man's face. His heart was racing in his chest. A sheet of foam latex came off in his hands and Angel looked back at the face of the man he'd seen in his dream.

"I don't like leaving a job unfinished.," the man said. "Once I'm through with you, I'll find Jamison."

Then the poison started taking over. Angel began hallucinating and went in and out of consciousness, then a severe thirst hit him. Now paralyzed, he slumped to the floor. Looking into the man's dark brown eyes, Angel prayed that Cal would somehow find his message…

The man reapplied his mask and took his time scouring the cabin to leave no trace. He didn't go through any of Ramirez's things, just simply packed everything up into his bag. Then, he poured himself a tall glass of Bourbon and sat in front of the stove, enjoying the amber liquid as he waited for his victim to finally die.

It was still dark and no one was about when the man left the cabin, carrying Ramirez's body over one shoulder. The empty thermos was now in a pocket of the victim's coat. In the half moonlight, as he came to the end of the dock, he could see there was a thin sheet of ice over the water. He quickly removed Ramirez's leg prosthesis and threw it into the lake, breaking up some of the ice. He'd been surprised to find his victim was still wearing his military tags, so he tossed them in as well. Then the man pushed the body into the lake – watching as it sank into the depths of the dark water.

It began to snow, which pleased him because it would cover his tracks. With all of his victim's belongings on the snowmobile, he drove back to the Sno-Park.

When he used Ramirez's keys to get into his vehicle, the man's cellphone buzzed. He looked down at a text on the screen and angrily exclaimed under his breath, "Damn it – not now! I'm not finished here…"

Angrily, he drove Ramirez's SUV to a remote area where it would not be found for some time.

CHAPTER 30

IT WAS EARLY ON New Year's Day when Micco sat at his desk working on his computer. For him, most holidays seemed to disappear these days. This was his usual routine every morning as he sipped his coffee before chores started on the ranch. And, if he wasn't working on the ranch, he was usually at his desk. Suddenly, he realized that he needed to get a life…or a girlfriend.

But, today Micco had a hangover. He tried to ignore the pounding in his head with more coffee and acetaminophen. Last night, downtown Bend had been one giant celebration bringing in the new year. With Cal gone, Micco was coerced to join a couple of their old high school buddies. The trio went bar-hopping without making any reservations. If there were seats at a bar, they'd stop, have a drink or two and some appetizers, and then move on to the next.

Their last stop was at the D&D. Micco liked seeing Hana, but she was so busy, there was no time for chatting. When Barney rang the bell at midnight, the place went wild. Hana was walking by with some drinks in her hands, but Micco impulsively stopped her to give her a quick kiss. That was the first time he'd ever done anything like that in his life and when he saw the surprised look on her face, he regretted it. He'd quickly put some bills on the bar and left immediately afterward.

Now, placing his throbbing head in his hands, Micco said to himself, "You idiot – you can do better than that!" He hadn't really had time to date much when he was in the service, so his experience with the opposite sex was pretty slim. He wasn't as smooth as Cal when it came to women.

Micco took a deep breath, shook his head, which he immediately regretted, and got back to work. His military background in Marine Communications gave him the skills to do some research that had helped Cal with his friend's murder last fall. He knew this would also come in handy for their new business adventure. But he did miss some of the great equipment he'd worked with in the service.

This was something neither of them had really done before, it was all innovative and exciting. Micco had arranged to get a DBA registered for the business name and all the PI documentation was complete. Cal understood the nuance of this type of work from his military training, so it was perfect for the pair of them.

The new landline he just had installed for the new business rang and he looked at his watch. It was 5:00 a.m. *Who the heck is calling at this hour?* he wondered, wincing at the shrill noise.

Micco cleared his throat and answered. "Triple A Detective Service."

"I'm Herman Casper and I need some immediate assistance," the voice on the other end said.

Micco could tell it was an older man and wrote the name down on a legal pad. "How can I help you?" he asked.

"I have a vandal at my house. It's been going on now for over a month, and I think I know who's doing it."

Micco rolled his eyes. He knew Cal wasn't going to like this type of case, but it was their first case.

"Let me take down some information, Mr. Casper, and I'll have our detective, Mr. Jamison, call you."

"It's got to be my dead brother's ghost doing these pranks. Charlie always liked to play tricks on me," the old man said.

When Micco heard this, he smiled, seeing the irony in the man's name. Suddenly, his headache was forgotten. "Please rest assured that Mr. Jamison will get to the bottom of this. He's…uh…out on another case right now, but should return in a day or so. I will need your address, sir…"

After he hung up, Micco remembered the first spy kit he begged his dad to get for him when he was in grade school. He thought of all the surveillance and possible stakeout tools they'd need for this kind of case and got on his computer to order some to arrive the next day. Understanding that they had to somewhat stay within the law, they might need small video cameras and audio recorders.

Then, he excitedly went online to get some tools for paranormal hunting. He'd always wanted to search for ghosts, which he fully believed in.

Micco's culture revered and honored past ancestors and trusted their spirits to guide the living. More than once in his life he'd felt that some elder had steered him on a better path, which he'd been thankful for. The Northern Paiute tribe believed that there were two souls in a man, one that died when the body died and the other that wandered. He thought of Mr. Casper's dead brother.

A FEW HOURS LATER, there was a knock on his door. Micco yelled, "It's open," and completed a credit card payment for some night goggles.

"Hi, Micco," a slender man said as he entered and closed the door. A blast of cold air followed him.

Micco looked up and smiled. Andy Shaw was a good friend of Cal's; they'd even played football together in high school. He worked for the local sheriff's office, was married with three kids and lived in the west end of Bend.

"Well, Detective Shaw, what're you doing out and about on a holiday?" Micco asked.

"I was just wondering if you've heard from Cal." Andy looked hopefully around the large open room.

"He's probably in the air somewhere as we speak. There's coffee if you want some."

Andy went to the kitchen and poured a cup.

Micco looked at the man and said, "I thought you were joining the State Police."

"Nah, I found that I'd have to move to Salem for the job and I can't do that to my family. I'm staying here."

Micco nodded. "I get it. By the way, I planned to visit the sheriff's office tomorrow, so you've saved me a trip."

"What about?"

Grabbing his empty coffee cup, Micco got up and walked to the kitchen. "Did Cal tell you why he flew his own plane back to North Carolina?"

Andy shook his head. "Not really, but I was really surprised he did that to report back to duty."

"Well, Cal is retiring from the military."

"No way!" Andy yelled as he sat down on one of the stools by the counter.

Micco winced and put his hand to his head. "Not so loud, man, I'm still hungover from last night."

Andy nodded and smiled. "Yeah, I heard about your little adventure with the guys." He took a sip of the dark liquid and said, "I never thought Cal would ever leave the Marines after all this time."

"Most of it's because of the hardship on Glenn at the ranch right now." Micco looked sharply at Andy and added, "But don't tell the old man I said that. I'm helping where I can."

The detective nodded. "Family first."

"You know Cal is a multi-tasker. Besides helping here on the ranch, he's starting a new PI business." Micco puffed out his chest as he leaned against the refrigerator. "And, I'm his assistant."

"Wow, I guess that makes sense. You both have the training for it."

"So, I was wondering if you think the sheriff might use Cal as a possible consultant on some cases – after he gets back. Maybe you could remind Scott Morrow that Cal was a cadet there during his high school years and how much help he was on Luther's case."

Andy shook his head. "I'm not sure, but I'll see what I can do to maybe make that happen. When did you last hear from Cal?"

"Yesterday, he was snowed in in Omaha. Should be back in a day or two."

"What's he doing in Nebraska?"

Micco shrugged. "I have no idea."

CHAPTER 31

AT THE JAMISON RANCH, Nina walked from her bedroom, tucking the back of her blouse into her jeans. She was still in her sock feet and was heading to the kitchen to make coffee. It had been a long night with little sleep. It was a new year, but ever since Cal left, she hadn't gotten a decent night's sleep, which was usual when he'd fly anywhere.

As she passed by a framed Jamison family tree hanging on the hallway wall, she stopped. Seeing the names of her husband's ancestors going back decades since their immigration from Scotland to America in 1802 filled her with nostalgia. John's family of in-laws had come from all over – France, Indiana, and San Francisco, either by boat, wagon, or train. She remembered the story that Glenn used to tell of how their eldest ancestor's wife had come on a ship from New Orleans, through the Panama Canal to Fort Astoria to meet her husband.

Then, she looked at her own small immediate family tree with her marriage to John and their four strong-willed sons. She was proud of each one of them, even if they were stubborn and all seemed to be going in different directions. It broke her heart when Cal pulled away from the family.

Nina sighed as she looked at their only daughter's name. Winona died of pneumonia at 2 months old. They had named her after Nina's dead grandmother, but called the little one 'Nonie.' She had wished for another daughter when she became pregnant again, but Tate was the spitting image of her husband.

Her marriage had been happy as she and her husband watched their sons grow as young boys. Yet, she always felt cheated. John had survived Vietnam, but their life together had been cut short when he was killed by someone unknown here on the ranch.

Saddened now by the memories, she walked into the kitchen and turned on the light. Nina had remodeled the cabinets and counters years ago in an attempt to bring the ancestral home more into the twenty-first century. It had been a little difficult since the interior walls were made of logs, but the carpenter she hired was brilliant, including updating the wiring for some of her newer appliances. She added a large island in the center of the room, which gave her more storage.

While the coffee brewed, she thought of her parents, Jim and Joan Bosch. They still lived on the family cattle ranch in Malheur County, near Vale, Oregon. Her stubborn father was so angry and disowned her when they found out she'd gotten pregnant before marriage. They hadn't seen each other in thirty-nine years and her parents had never met her sons. Nina realized that she had made the right choice to defy her father and marry John Jamison.

Her spirits lifted when she heard an airplane flying overhead and went outside. She held a hand over her eyes and when she saw it looked like Cal's plane, her heart leaped. She saw him circle over the family cemetery where all the Jamisons were buried. Even though he'd pulled away, she knew that he honored his heritage and loved this land, but she also understood Cal never let go of his father's death.

Cal was so much like her husband and she missed them both terribly. She knew Cal was angry with her and Jack about their decisions for the ranch, but he didn't know their reasons. Maybe it was time to bring him on board.

CHAPTER 32

FLYING OVER THE LARGE ranch he used to call home, Cal loved that it was mostly covered in a blanket of snow. The mountains were so beautiful this time of year. He was thankful his brother, Tate, had cleared the landing strip like he'd asked when he called the night before from his last stop in Jerome, Idaho.

The ranch's airplane, a C-185 Skywagon, stood under the open hangar. Cal and his dad used to fly that plane over the open ranges, dropping feed to their cattle. Thoughts surged through his mind as he circled around, checking some of the herd in a protected canyon - not far from where his dad was shot. He realized how much he missed his father. There were so many things he wanted to talk over with him, to get his advice, but knew that would never happen again. At that moment, Cal decided he would put everything he could into finding out more about his father's murder.

He banked his plane and flew over the area that was the old homestead, originally claimed by his namesake, Callum Jamison, in the 1820s. Callum was a brave young

Scot who came west after his parents immigrated to become a fur trader. He'd worked with the Peter Skene Ogden crew of what was sometimes called 'mountain men' before he decided to stay in Oregon. A few of the original small log cabins he'd built were still standing as a testament to his ancestry.

"What the hell, Jack?" Cal exclaimed when he saw that the old sawmill had been torn down. That mill had sustained his family for generations before they switched to raising cattle. He knew it had to be his brother, Jack, who had destroyed it.

WITH ANGER IN HIS heart, Cal landed the plane and went to the barn in search of his asshole brother. He found Jack cleaning one of the horse stalls. Without saying a word, he jumped his younger brother and the two men began to fight. Years of pent-up emotions surfaced as they rolled to the ground, pounding on each other. Their other brothers, Tate and Clyde ran into the barn and tried to break them up, but they just got pulled into the brawl themselves. Before they knew it, the four brothers were in a free-for-all.

Wes came into the barn with Nina and just watched with their arms crossed over their chests. They looked at each other, knowing that these young men needed to get it all out of their systems until they were exhausted. This wasn't the first time this had happened. Slowly, one by one, each man pulled out of the pile and stood up. Cal and Jack were the last two still fighting.

"Mom!" Clyde exclaimed as he tried to tuck in his disheveled shirt.

That broke the other brothers up. All four stood in a line, bruised and bloody, and looked at their mother.

"Clean yourselves up and meet me in the house," she said. "It's time we all talked." Nina turned and walked out of the barn.

CHAPTER 33

CAL WAS STILL FUMING as he flew his plane back to the Double J. His mother's words sat heavily on his mind as he tried to make sense of it all. He was filled with guilt, knowing that he was mostly to blame since he had ignored Jack's calls for so long. Maybe there was something he could've done to prevent such a drastic change.

He shook his head as he landed on the cleared airstrip, hearing his grandfather's words before he'd left. *You may have to face him one day*, Glenn had said.

Gathering his things, Cal walked toward the house. He saw his grandmother wearing a purple wool coat and scarf. She was near a fence, feeding a snack to her favorite Belted Galloway cow she called 'Cookie Monster.' As Cal waved to her, he took a deep breath and wondered what he was going to tell his grandfather.

Winnie hugged him. "We're so glad you're home."

"Me, too," he said and hugged Winnie. "I missed everyone."

Glenn and Micco came out of the barn and Cal went to meet them.

"Happy New Year, son!" Glenn exclaimed.

Cal leaned in and softly said to the two men, "You're both going to want to hear this."

IN THE KITCHEN, CAL explained to Glenn and his friend about the Jamison Ranch financial issues. "It looks like the land is bleeding money that is not coming back in." He took a deep breath and added, "Jack got Mom to sign some papers to change acres of the land use where the old sawmill stood. He's going to build a guest resort in that area to bring in money."

"Over my dead body!" Glenn exclaimed as he jumped up so quickly, that his chair fell back to the floor and his face started turning red.

Cal tried to calm him down. "Remember your blood pressure, Glenn. Sit down and I'll get you some water."

Micco silently picked up the chair and helped Glenn sit back down.

"My grandad built that water-powered sawmill before I was born," Glenn said sadly. "Fergus designed his like Ewing Young's mill on Chehalem Creek in the Willamette Valley. Young was another fur trader, like our ancestor that started our clan here in Oregon."

Cal hated that he had more bad news as he waited for his grandfather to take a few sips of water. "I'm sorry to report that the mill is already gone."

Glenn stared out the window for a few moments, the clock over the sink ticking away the seconds. "I know I've said I always hated that mill," the old man said as he put his head in his hands, "how they took out so many trees and changed the landscape, but it was always a part of our history."

"Yes, I know," Cal said in a soft voice, trying to calm

his grandfather whose Scottish blood was very easy to rile.

Then, Glenn got up and paced the room, talking about their ancestors surviving for decades, only to see it falling into ruin. "The changes made to our heritage over the years just keep chiseling away at the dream of Callum Jamison."

"That's why I left, too," Cal said.

"I can't believe it." Anger rising again, Glenn pounded his fist on the heirloom table that had come on a ship by the first Callum's wife's family. "This never would've happened with your father in charge!"

"I know," Cal said again, stroking his grandfather's arm. He looked at Micco for answers.

After a few seconds, Micco offered, "I can check with my dad to see if he knows what else they're planning at the Jamison."

That seemed to calm Glenn a little. "Wes is a good man," he said. "He was always an ally for me, ever since he became foreman. Besides, he's Winnie's second cousin."

Cal hated the defeated look in his grandfather's eyes but was glad when Winnie entered the kitchen.

"What's all this?" she asked.

Cal went to his grandmother and said, "Glenn will explain everything."

AFTER GLENN WAS MUCH calmer, Cal and Micco went up to the apartment above the garage. Cal sat at the small counter. A large whiteboard stood against one wall.

Micco went to the fridge and pulled out two beers. "I don't think it's too early for these," he said as he popped the tops.

"Agreed," Cal sighed and took a long sip. "What a bloody mess my family has created."

"I'm sure it will all get worked out." Micco set his beer

down and asked, "How did it go at Camp Lejeune?"

"My CO wanted me to join the Reserves, but I told him I have to think of my family first." He took another long sip.

"How did he take it?"

Cal smiled and said, "He did mention I could get recalled if they need me."

"So, how does it feel to be no longer on active duty?"

"Right now, it stinks. They've got some new intel about our bombing last year in Afghanistan, but the major wouldn't tell me anything."

Micco walked over to his desk and sat down. "Mary Cresswell started calling me now to find out where you are. You need to get a girlfriend, man, so they'll leave me alone!"

Cal sat on the couch and asked, "So, have you asked Hana out yet?"

Micco sidestepped the question by showing Cal his new PI license and ID.

"Where'd you get this photo?" Cal asked.

"Mary brought it over – it was the one she took that she used to paint that picture she gave you. I photoshopped your horse out."

Excitedly, Micco showed Cal all the new spy toys he'd bought. Then, he went to the whiteboard and turned it around. "I have our first case!"

Looking at the assignment sheet, Cal groaned. "Man, this is only a vandalism case."

"But, it's a start," Micco said as he pointed to the evidence he'd collected.

Cal walked to the board and looked over Micco's notes and articles that he'd researched. He pointed to a funny drawing under the 'Suspects' column. "What's this?"

Micco grinned and said, "Our client, Mr. Casper, thinks

it's his dead brother's ghost!"

CHAPTER 34

ANDY SHAW WAS DRIVING one of the county sheriff's trucks with Deputy Rupert Bateman by his side. They were following the wide tracks previously made by a Sno-Cat in the Cascade Lakes district of Central Oregon. Their vehicle was towing a trailer carrying a snowmobile, standard procedure for this type of incident.

"We very seldom get a report about an abandoned vehicle out here at Ten-mile Sno Park," Andy said. "Paulina Lake Lodge is near here."

"The State Police called it in this morning," Rupert said. "We sure had our share of reports come in for New Year's – DUIs, illegal fireworks, and gunshots fired off."

"Some people seem to go nuts on certain holidays."

As they approached the area, two men were standing near the tall Sno-Cat parked next to a gray SUV.

Rupert said, "Wow, that car is half covered in snow."

Smiling, Andy said, "It's just one storm away from being totally buried. And, you get to help the Sno-Cat guys to unbury it so you can get inside. Once you find the registration, call for one of our tow trucks to meet you at the substation in LaPine."

He ignored the angry look he got from Rupert as he wiped snow from the license plate with his gloved hand and jotted down the number in the notebook he always carried.

"What're you going to do?" the deputy shot back.

"I'm going to the lodge to investigate - since that's my job." He grinned and added, "You get to ride back with these men in the Sno-Cat hooked up to this vehicle." Andy liked ribbing Rupert because the guy had a burr up his butt about his best friend, Cal.

As they got out, there were a few other vehicles, but they only had small amounts of snowfall on them. This told Andy approximately how long the SUV had been there. He then removed the snowmobile from their trailer and waved to Rupert as he rode up the road toward the lodge.

AS ANDY PASSED THE gate to Paulina Lake, which was used during the winter months to prohibit traffic, he stopped on the small bridge, noting the icy stream now barely trickling. As he continued, he passed the old iconic red sleigh, then parked the vehicle at the main lodge building. On the right, the snow-covered boat ramp led out to the lake, which was almost totally frozen now.

When he saw the cabins in the trees, he thought of bringing his family sometime before all this changed. They hadn't been on a vacation together in a long time. His wife, Maureen, worked so hard at the hospital and his kids were starting to get to the ages when they didn't really like spending time with their parents.

Andy walked into the lodge's restaurant and approached the young man behind the registration desk. He shook his head when he saw the hippy guy with red hair behind the counter who reminded him of his brother-in-law.

"Hi there," the guy said. "I'm Bud Smithe, with an 'e.'"

Andy showed him his badge and said, "I'm Detective Shaw with the County Sheriff's Department, checking on an abandoned SUV up at Ten-mile Sno-Park. Can I see your registration book?"

Bud turned a large leather-bound book around so Andy could check the names. He was disappointed when he noted that guests did not have to register their vehicles when they checked in.

"Have you had any strange activity around here in the last few days?" Andy asked.

"Well, there was this one guy that checked in four days ago, but he never checked out." Bud pointed to Angel Ramirez's name. "He came in on a snowmobile. Some girl was looking for him - I guess they had a date or something. But when I went to check, his cabin was emptied and, man, he was just gone."

"What is the girl's name?" Andy asked and wrote Leslie's name and info down. "Is she still here?"

"Nope. She and her girlfriends checked out that next day after we found the guy was gone. I guess they had a flight to catch." Bud just smiled and added, "This happens a lot this time of year. Some people just can't handle our weather, but the guy paid in cash for a week."

CHAPTER 35

SISTERS, OREGON IS A city that was established in the 1880s where two wagon trails intersected and had grown into a large art community. It was named after the three peaks to the west – the locals call them Faith, Hope, and Charity. Most of the streets were cleared now from the last snowstorm.

Each June, when he was young, Cal would go to Sisters to ride in the annual rodeo. He knew Luther Greeves and his young son, Riley, also participated. Luther's death the previous year had been a strange case. Cal consulted with the sheriff on it while he was on medical leave from the Marines. Somehow, he thought that his new career would be more interesting than the case he had today.

Cal shook his head to clear his mind. He passed one of his favorite haunts, the Sisters Saloon, which used to be a hotel that opened in 1912. He preferred to sit in the bar, where old photos reminded him of a slower time in life. He decided to stop there later for lunch and have one of their famous Spanish Coffees before returning home.

This case bothered Cal as he followed his phone's GPS

to his first client's address. It was a large two-story log home that sat on a plot of land on the southern outskirts of the downtown area. In Sisters, two blocks from Main Street were considered the 'outskirts.'

The house faced east and a garden shed and greenhouse stood in the back. The entry was a large, high-ceilinged open area with oversized furniture and a western décor. Twp elk heads stared back at him from one of the walls.

As he interviewed the owner, Mr. Herman Casper, Cal tried to keep a straight face as the guy explained that he thought it was his twin brother's ghost doing the vandalism. He was glad he'd decided to come alone on this first visit.

The man was in his eighties, very thin with only a few strands of gray hair at his temples. He wore a polyester jogging suit and a portable oxygen tank sat next to his chair.

"My grandparents built this house in 1908," the old man said as he gasped for air. "Charlie, my twin brother, and I were born here in 1932."

He stopped for a moment and took in some oxygen, then continued. "My brother died from a car accident when he was seventy-eight."

The old man started to giggle, which brought on a coughing fit. After he finally caught his breath, he continued. "Charlie was full of piss and vinegar – always pulling pranks on me."

Now Cal fully understood why Micco had been so excited about his new paranormal equipment and his infatuation with the supernatural. "How long has this been going on?" he asked.

"For three months now – ever since our birthday last October."

"Tell me exactly what has happened here," Cal said as he took out a notebook. He knew he'd remember the details but found that most people liked it when their statements were being written down.

"Most of it is in the backyard. Plants were taken from my greenhouse, and interestingly, they'd be replaced with something else later. I grow vegetables there all year."

Cal wondered how the old man was able to even make it to the greenhouse in his condition but remained silent.

"Also, other stuff goes missing, like the gnomes that I've had for years - bird feeders, too. Later, I'd find both the gnomes and feeders in a different place in the yard. And, last summer and fall, the fountain was emptied almost every night."

Cal waited a moment to see if Mr. Casper had more to add. He did.

"Sometimes, I'll find something is fixed, like my snow blower that's been broken for ten years. My brother always took care of that kind of stuff."

"You don't use the blower, do you?"

"Not anymore."

"Does anything happen inside the house?"

Mr. Casper thought for a moment, then shook his head. "It's mostly in the backyard."

"I'd like to take a look around if that's okay," Cal said. "Also, is there a room I could use, preferably one that is upstairs with a window looking out over the yard?"

"Yes, there is a small loft on the back side of the house. It was our playroom when we were boys."

THAT NIGHT, WITH A full moon overhead, Cal was in the upstairs room near the back window, watching both the yard and computer screen that Micco had set up. Multiple camera views showed on the monitor. The room the old man called the 'loft' was the attic, dusty and cob-webbed. There were boxes everywhere and some toys, like the wooden rocking horse, were left from when the Casper boys were small.

Earlier that day, Micco had installed a video camera on a telephone pole to get a wide-angle view of the greenhouse and tool shed. Cal smiled when he'd asked Micco to dress in a lineman's uniform so the neighbors wouldn't worry. His friend had also added microphones and motion-activated cameras and lights around the yard for what he called his 'ghost' detection. Micco was totally in his element on this case.

Cal's stomach growled and he couldn't wait for Micco to get back with dinner. He thought of Mr. Casper's comment about his brother's pranks and remembered the ones he and Micco did on each other when they were young while living at the Jamison Ranch. He smiled when he thought of the prank he had set up for when his friend arrived.

Micco climbed up the narrow stairs with some burgers and fries. "I brought some to old Mr. Casper, too." He looked at all the spy equipment he'd set up and said excitedly, "Wow, our first stakeout!"

The aroma of the food was too hard to resist. Cal opened the bag, pulled out a burger, and sat in a chair near the window. "Earlier, I talked to some of the neighbors, but no one else around here seems to have these things happening to them. Not sure if any of them are suspects yet."

"Then why is this old guy being targeted like this – maybe it is his brother."

Cal laughed and said, "Dude, I don't think this is a ghost. There has to be someone else behind these shenanigans. And what ghost goes around fixing equipment or replacing plants?"

Micco opened a canvas bag he'd left before and pulled out a hand-held tool.

"What's that?" Cal asked.

"My thermal-imaging camera!" Micco plugged the device into the computer and turned it on. "I'll be able to see any hot spots in the yard with this baby."

Cal shook his head and dug into his burger. He patiently waited for the right moment. To kill time, he talked about wanting to go fly fishing when the season opened in April.

Micco smiled. "Remember how often you snagged yourself in the butt with a fly hook while learning how to use that damned thing?"

"I've gotten much better since then."

At that moment, Cal pushed 'Play' on the computer and an eerie wailing sound filled the attic.

"What the..." Micco said, jumping up. He ran to the window, then back to the computer. "Did we just catch a ghost?"

Cal laughed so hard he almost fell out of his chair. "Relax, pal. I downloaded an audio file I found earlier just to spook you. You're way too serious about this ghost."

HOURS LATER, AFTER MIDNIGHT, Cal had turned off the lights in the room and was watching through a pair of binoculars that somehow Micco had connected to the computer. The full moon caught a pair of small images moving in the snow. Zooming in, Cal said, "I was right! It's "Trash Pandas" as Glenn likes to call them."

"Raccoons?" Micco said.

"Take a look for yourself."

Looking at the monitor, Micco said, "Dang, those are big ones. That's probably how the fountain was drained."

"Exactly," Cal said. "One mystery solved."

Micco moved the camera to one side of the yard and jumped back. "Check this out!" he said.

On the small screen, Cal saw that there was definitely something causing heat in the yard. He went to the window. Through the binoculars, he could see a tall figure in tan clothes moving through the darkness.

"Come on!" Cal whispered and the two men grabbed their coats and left the attic.

OUTSIDE, CAL WENT LEFT and Micco went right, circling around the figure that was now near the greenhouse. Cal jumped and the figure faceplanted in the snow. He turned the figure over and saw that it was a woman in camouflage clothes.

"Get off of me," the woman yelled, trying to fight off her attacker.

"Stop!" Cal said and brought her up to her feet. "Who the hell are you?"

The woman stood at attention, her hands behind her back and feet sternly planted. Cal knew the stance. "You're military?" he asked.

"Yes, sir," she replied. 'Well, I was…before my medical discharge. I'm Bonnie Couch."

By now, all of Micco's paranormal equipment had turned on and the entire backyard was flooded with light.

Mr. Casper came out onto the back porch, shaded his eyes and yelled, "Is that Charlie?"

Cal looked at Micco, who understood and went to calm the old man down and get him back inside. He then turned back to the woman who was shivering and wringing her ungloved red hands. He took off his coat and placed it over her shoulders.

"Where were you stationed, Bonnie?" Cal asked softly.

"I was in Desert Storm before I got out."

Cal could see the fear in her eyes, which kept looking around as if someone else was about to attack.

"So, you've been doing the vandalism here in Mr. Casper's yard since last fall?"

"I only took some food from the greenhouse – I'm a vegetarian. But I always tried to put something back when I did."

Micco returned. "What about the missing gnomes?" he asked.

"Some kids used to sneak in here just after I started coming around. I followed them and brought the statues back." She began shivering. "Am I going to be arrested? I won't do well in jail."

Cal recognized her PTSD symptoms.

"I'm Cal Jamison," he said, then turned to his friend. "And this is my sidekick, Micco. We were hired by the owner to find out who was doing this damage to his property. But, under the circumstances, I think I can convince Mr. Casper to not press charges."

Bonnie relaxed a bit and said, "Oh, thank you, sir."

"Where are you staying?"

She nodded behind her. "I've got a small tent back in the woods…I don't really have a home."

"Any family?"

She looked down at the snow and said, "No, sir."

He thought for a moment, then said, "I think I have a place for you to stay – at least for a while. And don't call me 'sir.' My name is Cal."

CHAPTER 36

CAL WALKED INTO THE Double J house after helping Micco stow all of his equipment. In the living room, in front of a warm fire, Bonnie sat with Winnie on the couch and Glenn was in the kitchen pouring hot chocolate into some mugs on a tray.

On the way to the ranch, Cal had asked Bonnie about her medical discharge, explaining his own recent leave. She'd told him about an attack on their Army base in Iraq that left her with major internal injuries. Her dad was military, killed in action in Vietnam. Her mom died shortly afterward. That's when she entered the Army.

After Bonnie had finished, Cal felt secure that no harm would come to his family and he knew that his grandparents would open their home to her.

Winnie handed Bonnie a tightly woven, conical-shaped basket with bands of maroon-colored geometric designs. "This has been in my family for generations," she said proudly. "I am of the Northern Paiute Tribe that lives on the Warm Springs Reservation. My grandmother made this and used it for gathering wild herbs and seeds for our family. I use it now when I work in my garden."

"I love to garden," Bonnie said. She turned the basket over and then gently handed it back to Winnie. "This is beautifully made." Tears came to her eyes as she said, "You have all been so kind. I'm not used to this type of hospitality."

Glenn came out, carrying the tray of drinks. "Tell us a bit about yourself, Bonnie. Our boy here is a Marine. He said you were also military."

Bonnie quickly wiped her eyes and stood by the fire. "Like I told Cal, in the Army, I trained as a helicopter repairer. I was among some of the first women to be allowed to be deployed to the Persian Gulf during Desert Storm and I worked on Cobras and Black Hawks."

Cal said, "I recently met a guy in Red Cloud, Nebraska who was a Black Hawk helicopter pilot over there – Ken Whitaker—"

"Oh my God," Bonnie exclaimed, "I can't believe it - I knew Ken! I always wondered if he didn't have a crush on me."

"I have his information."

"Where was your home, dear?" Winnie asked.

"I grew up on a farm in Oklahoma. My dad taught me how to fix almost anything."

Glenn smiled. "Well, Bonnie, do you know anything about tractors? I've got one that's on the blink and now's a good time to get it running."

She smiled and said, "I think I can help with that, sir."

Winnie went to stand by Bonnie. "Won't your family be worried about you?"

"No, I don't have any family anymore."

"What brought you here to Oregon?" Cal asked.

Bonnie smiled, thankful for the change in the conversation. "A friend in helicopter training came from here. When I got out, I decided to look her up, but she's moved and I don't know where she is now. So, I guess I'm on my own."

"Not anymore," Glenn said smiling.

Winnie took Bonnie's hand. "It's getting late. We're about the same size and I have some extra clothes that should fit you. Come with me." The two women walked down the hall.

ALONE, CAL TOLD HIS grandfather about his decision to leave the military and become an investigator.

"I can't believe you did that – after all these years." Glenn hugged his grandson. "But I will say I am relieved that you won't be disappearing on those dangerous missions anymore."

Cal didn't tell him about the possible recall option. He then said, "I think I'll check with Jamie Greeves to see if Bonnie can stay at their place to help out since Luther's gone."

Glenn nodded. "Just don't take her away until she fixes my tractor." He finished his cocoa and said, "So now you're one of those private eyes."

"Yep," Cal said as he sat on the couch. "I thought I could do something with all the training the military gave me. But mostly, I plan to work around here doing a few of the chores, if you'll let me."

"I'll appreciate your help, son." Glenn gathered the mugs and returned to the kitchen.

Micco came in and stood in front of the fire with his hands on his hips and said, "Really? You introduce me as your sidekick? I need a different title if we're going to do this business together."

Cal smiled as he looked up at his friend. "How about

'Technical Assistant?'"

"That's better."

"So," Cal said, as he stretched his legs in front of him. "I'm wondering how much we made for solving this case."

Micco handed Cal a check from Mr. Casper. "Your first paid job as a PI!"

Cal looked at the check and laughed. "Well, at least we've got beer money!"

CHAPTER 37

IT WAS A SATURDAY when Andy glanced at the address report on the abandoned SUV found near Paulina Lake - a gray GMC Yukon. The vehicle was registered to Darren Lions who still lived with his parents in the Larkspur neighborhood of Bend, an area with trails leading to the Pilot Butte cinder cone.

The day before, Andy ran a background check on Darren and his family and found that Darren was in the Army Reserves and recently spent time in Afghanistan. His Facebook page had photos going back years when the Lions family sponsored two exchange students.

Andy parked his county vehicle at the long, yellow ranch-style home with two big trucks and a motorhome parked on one side. He picked up his notepad and walked up to the door. Some of the paint was starting to peel near the doorbell, which had one of those surveillance cameras attached. Before he could push the button, an older man wearing a T-shirt and denim overalls opened it.

"What do you want?" the man with the two-day-old beard asked gruffly.

Andy knew that Pete Lions was trouble, arrested numerous times for bar fights. He took out his badge and said, "My name is Detective Andy Shaw with the County Sheriff's Office. I'm here to report that we found your son's vehicle."

"Come on in," the man said disgustedly and turned away.

The vestibule opened into a large living room with overstuffed furniture. A football game between the Broncos and the Chiefs was on a big-screen TV. The heavy smell of beer and cigarette smoke was overpowering.

A dark-haired man in his late twenties sat in one of the La-Z-Boy chairs, watching the game as he drank from a can of craft beer called "Pete's Wicked Ale." Andy knew the beer had been discontinued a few years back.

A woman, carrying a small baby, entered the room and sat down on the couch. She was about Darren's age, but Andy could see the family resemblance and noticed no wedding ring on her finger.

"Get up, son," Pete said as he kicked the foot of the young man's chair and muted the TV. "The cops are here."

"Hi Darren," Andy said. "I'm Andy Shaw with the Sheriff's Office. Your SUV was found near Paulina Lake yesterday."

"How the hell did it get there?" the old man yelled.

Darren shrugged and shook his head. "I got no idea."

"What's going on?" the woman asked but was ignored by her father.

"What is your name, Miss?" Andy asked.

"Michelle, I'm Darren's sister."

"Get on with it," the old man yelled at the detective.

Andy cleared his throat and took out his notepad and pen. "What do you do for a living, Darren?" he asked, even though he already knew the answer.

"After I got back from overseas, I took over Dad's job when he retired as a driver for Les Schwab. Each morning I pick up a truck and cargo at the Redmond Airport air freight terminal. Then, I deliver everything to various Schwab tire centers around here."

Andy made a few notes, then asked, "If you take a Schwab truck for deliveries, do you have any idea how your personal vehicle could've ended up at that Sno-Park?"

Darren looked at his dad before answering. "No, I always leave it at the airport while I'm doing my deliveries. The center in LaPine is usually my last stop."

"I read that you had two exchange students here in the past – a girl and a boy. Are you still in contact with these people?"

"How'd you find that out?" Darren asked.

"Social media," Andy replied.

Michelle answered, "Maria was great. I even visited her in Spain before my baby was born. We're still friends and we email every so often."

Andy looked at Darren, but he shook his head. "I lost touch after Bo left. That's what we called him, anyway. He was from Turkey."

"What's this got to do with my son's GMC?" the dad roared.

"I'm just curious. Why was the vehicle never reported stolen?" Andy asked.

Darren looked again at his dad. "After my last delivery a few days ago, I had to call Dad to come to get me at work since my rig was missing at the terminal—"

Pete cut in, "We just figured it was some kids messing around…we were going to report it today."

CHAPTER 38

CAL DROVE HIS JEEP into Bend to meet Micco for lunch. The temperature was somewhat warmer than the previous month, but there were still some snowflakes flurrying around.

At a stoplight on Bond Street, he looked over and saw another Jeep like his and called out to the driver, "We recognize perfection!" The other man honked, then raced ahead after the light turned green.

Cal parked in front of the D&D, and walked in. Micco was already at the bar, so he joined his friend.

"You were out early this morning," Micco said.

"Bonnie asked me to pick up some parts for a front-end loader and the Redmond store was the only one who carried them."

"She seems to be working out okay at Jamie's, even though she prefers to sleep in the barn."

Cal nodded. "After all she's been through, I totally understand."

Hana came over to take Cal's order. She set a cup of coffee in front of him that had a photo of a big fish on it. It was Cal's favorite mug. "Our special today is meatloaf," she said as she eyed Micco.

"I'll take the meatloaf," Cal said smiling.

After the small waitress left, he said to Micco, "Okay, man, if you don't ask Hana out, I will on your behalf."

Just then, a woman with dark hair came in and hugged Cal. "You're back!"

"Hi, Mary," Cal turned and saw the woman he'd dated a few times. "What're you doing here?"

"Picking up an order. I'm working at the gallery today." She waved to Hana.

"I thought you were going back to Seattle," Cal said.

Mary sat on the stool next to him. "I was going to, but because of Jamie's news, I'll be staying a while longer."

"What news?" Cal asked.

Mary leaned in closer and softly told the two men about her sister's surgery scheduled the next day. "I'm not sure she would appreciate me telling you, but I think she needs all the friends she can get right now."

Cal said, "If there's anything I can do, just let me know."

"I wouldn't mind if you came to the hospital to wait with me," she said.

"Just let me know what time and I'll be there."

Hana brought Mary's order. After she paid, Mary looked at her watch, got up and said, "I have to run."

After she left, Micco smiled at Cal. "That woman is like a whirlwind."

Still standing by Micco at the end of the bar, Hana nodded. "I like her. Oh, by the way, Cal, Larry, our temporary bartender, told me that some guy was in the day you left asking about you."

"Did Larry find out who it was?"

"No, he couldn't really describe the guy, either."

Cal looked at Micco and said, "Larry's no help."

Hana nodded, then leaned in toward Micco and said softly, "So, will you have lunch with me tomorrow? It's my day off."

Surprised, Micco looked at Cal who raised his hands as if he had nothing to do with her asking. Then, flashing a smile, Micco said, "Sure."

CHAPTER 39

"I HATE THESE GOWNS," Jamie said to the nurse as she tried to sit up in the hospital bed.

"I know." Maureen Shaw smiled as she prepped Jamie for her surgery. "I wish they'd let us nurses design them."

"You're Andy's wife, aren't you? He and Cal Jamison are good friends."

The woman with the pink streak in her brown hair smiled. "Yes, Andy and I've been married now for sixteen years. My sweet twin boys are in the seventh grade now."

"I like your hair," Jamie said in an attempt to avoid the reason she was in the hospital.

As Maureen fluffed Jamie's pillow, she smiled. "Thank you. Our fifteen-year-old daughter did this for me. I wanted to do something different – thank God it's only temporary. Dr. Bello likes it, too. She's one of my favorite surgeons here at St. Charles. Did you know the original hospital was built in Bend in the early 1900s on what was called 'Hospital Hill?' Over the years, it's grown into a major medical system throughout the county. We have a great trauma center here now."

Jamie smiled and said, "I know you're just trying to distract and calm me and it's working. I love the history of our area."

"Me, too."

"Is there anything I need to know for after the surgery?" Jamie asked. "I was in a daze when my doctor went over it in her office."

"That's normal," Maureen said. "You will be in recovery for a while, then once you're awake, I'll bring your family in to see you." Seeing the panic again in Jamie's eyes, she touched her patient's hand and said, "Let's wait and see, but I'm sure you will be fine."

MARY SAT WITH CAL in the waiting room. "I'm so glad you're here," she sighed. "I don't like hospitals."

"Only the medical staff like hospitals," Cal said with a smile. He was glad he'd brought coffee when he arrived.

"Bonnie is with the kids." Mary looked at Cal and added, "She is a great help around the ranch. Thank you so much for bringing her to us."

"I'm just happy it's all working out for everyone."

Mary took a deep sip from her coffee. Then, she turned to Cal and said, "I'm concerned about Riley. He's gotten into trouble for fighting another boy and is now grounded. He's pretty angry. Would you mind talking to him?"

"Not at all," Cal said. "I could go there today after Jamie's surgery."

"Also, there's something wrong with Champ, Luther's horse."

"I'll call the vet, for you."

Mary put her hand on Cal's. "We appreciate all your help. It means so much to us." Then, she held her coffee in both hands, took another sip and said, "I didn't get a chance to tell you that I went back to the Jamison Ranch to get more rocks for my paints. I actually had dinner with your mother…and your brother, Jack."

Cal frowned, not sure how he felt about her meeting his family. "He's a piece of work."

"Jack was very nice and took me horseback riding down by the river." Mary sighed and added, "It was a good day."

Just then, Dr. Bello came out and walked to them. "The surgery went well. After a while, Jamie will start radiation, but she will be able to return to work as early as next week. I don't think she will need chemotherapy."

"Oh, what good news. Thank you so much, Doctor," Mary said. "When can I see her?"

"The nurse will come get you as soon as she's awake."

Cal was surprised to see his brother coming into the waiting area. Jack went up to Mary, took one hand, and asked how her sister was. It was the first time Cal had seen his brother ever interested in anything other than the ranch. Feeling like a third wheel, he said goodbye to Mary and left.

CHAPTER 40

DRIVING UP THE LANE to Luther and Jamie's house brought back the trauma this family had gone through. Cal knew that Jamie's parents had given the place to her and Luther after they were married and took Mary with them to New York. The girls' parents died in an auto accident in 2008. Then Luther's violent death the previous year in that burning bush. This family had seen enough tragedy.

As he approached the open barn door, Duke, the old coonhound, came running out, baying a greeting. Cal saw Bonnie and Riley standing near Luther's horse that was tethered in the aisle, one hind leg cocked up onto the toe. Little Josie was petting her pony's nose at a stall farther down in the barn. Cal got out, rubbed the dog's head, and went to the back of his Jeep to get a box of some additional machinery parts Bonnie needed.

"Hi all," he said as he walked toward them and laid the container inside the door.

"Uncle Cal," Josie screamed and ran into his arms. She'd called him 'uncle' for years, even though they weren't really related.

"Hello Cal," Bonnie said.

Riley didn't say anything. He was looking at the horse's left hind leg.

"Your mom's surgery went well," Cal told them. "I think she'll be home soon."

"That's good news," Bonnie said and took Josie in her arms.

Cal said more to Riley than the others, "I heard that Champ isn't well. Mary asked me to call Doc Thompson, so he's on his way."

"We can manage," Riley snapped back.

"I got those parts you needed, Bonnie," Cal said to ease some of the tension.

Bonnie thanked him, then came closer to Cal and told him that Jamie told her the horse had been lethargic since Luther's death. "I'm going to take Josie into the house for a snack," she said and left with the little girl.

Cal went over to Riley and asked, "So what do you think is wrong with Champ?"

"Don't know for sure."

Lifting the horse's hind leg, Cal looked to see if there was anything in the hoof, but it was clean.

"I already did that," Riley snapped again.

Cal released the leg and looked at the boy. "Okay, Riley, you've got to tell me why you're so pissed off."

The teenager looked at him with his hands on his hips. "Because life sucks!" Then, he walked to a hay bale and sat down.

"Your Aunt Mary told me you were grounded."

"That asshole Travis started the fight in the mall. He's been jealous of me ever since we started riding in rodeos. I always beat his barrel racing time with my horse, Sherlock."

At the mention of his name, a sorrel Quarter Horse in a stall across the aisle popped his head over the gate and whinnied for attention.

"Your dad always said your horse was bred to cut cattle from a herd."

Riley nodded. "Now, I'm the one stuck here and I can't go anywhere."

"You'll be a senior this fall in high school," Cal said in an attempt to lighten the mood. "Any ideas about college yet?"

Shrugging his shoulders, Riley said, "Mom wants me to go to the University of Oregon, but I don't know..."

Cal noticed a photo pinned on one wall of Luther with Roy Masterson, a guy who did impressive rope tricks on and off his horse. "When was this taken?"

"I took it on one of our rodeo trips to Pendleton. After we got home, Dad started teaching me a few of those moves." Riley took a deep breath and looked away. "I miss my dad…"

Cal sat down on a bale across the aisle from the boy. He could see Riley was about to cry but was trying hard not to show it. "I understand…I was your age when I lost my dad."

Riley looked up. "I never knew that. How did he die?"

"He was shot while working on some fence at our ranch. We still don't know what happened. At least you know about your dad. You have some closure."

The young boy thought for a moment. "That doesn't make it any easier. And, now Mom's sick."

"She's getting better. And your aunt is going to be here for a while longer, too."

"How did you deal with losing your dad," Riley asked. "I just see red anytime I think about it."

"I kept busy," Cal answered. "I had to find a way to move on. I know it's hard, but it does get easier with time." He leaned forward with his elbows on his knees and looked into Riley's eyes. "Eventually, I realized my dad is never really gone…he's always in my thoughts. Whenever I got sad thinking about him, I'd try to remember some fun time we had together, like when we would go fly fishing. What was a fun time you had with your dad?"

Riley stared at the ground. Eventually, he looked up and said, "I loved being at the rodeo with him."

Cal smiled and said, "Your dad was a superstar in the arena."

"That's the only place I still feel connected to him. I'm training for next summer's rodeo in Sisters."

"Hang on to those memories and your dad will always be with you."

A VAN WITH THE logo of a horse on the side pulled into the lane.

Cal got up and said, "Doc Thompson's here."

As the older man parked the vehicle near the barn door and got out, he gave Cal a knowing look. On the phone earlier, the two men had arranged to work together to help Riley with his issues.

"Hello you two," Doc said as he pushed up his wire-rimmed glasses. He grabbed his black bag and walked into the barn.

"Hey, Doc," Cal responded.

Champ started whinnying loudly and pawed at the ground with his front hoof.

"Hello, old man," Doc cooed to the Gypsy Cob horse he'd known since Luther bought him years ago.

"You didn't need to come," Riley said as he went protectively to the white and black animal. "I've got everything in hand."

Silently, the men watched as the boy started talking

softly to the horse as he pulled an ice pack from a nearby cooler and wrapped it around the hock joint. Immediately, the animal began to calm down. The men knew that last fall, Champ had been attacked by a Cougar at the camp near the Badlands where Luther was killed. Cal wondered if there wasn't some injury leftover from that event that could be the problem, but didn't say anything.

Doc walked up near Riley and said, "Has he been ridden lately?"

"I try to exercise him whenever I can, but I stopped as soon as I noticed he was favoring his leg."

"You did the right thing. Usually, when they stand like this – with their leg cocked up onto the toe, it indicates a possible injury or trauma. He hasn't had a fall, has he?" Doc asked Riley as he examined the horse.

"Not that I know of, but I think he's just missing Dad."

Cal and Doc looked at each other.

"That could be the case," Doc said, "but that doesn't explain his behavior." He continued to check the leg. After a moment, he gazed at Riley and asked, "May I remove this for a moment?"

When Riley nodded, Doc unwrapped the hock for a closer look. "I was concerned that he may have a stone or possibly cut his hoof, but there's no bruising there."

"That's the first thing I checked," Riley said.

"He does have some swelling and heat in the hock. Your ice pack is spot on." Doc rewrapped the leg and he gingerly stood up. "It's hard to tell until I've done more tests, but I think this could simply be arthritis related. After all, he is over fifteen years old – that's almost fifty in human years."

When Cal saw Riley's face, he added, "I'm sure he'll get well again." He knew the boy couldn't handle another loss right now. "He just may need to take it a little easy for a while."

Doc nodded and added, "There's no cure for arthritis." Then, he laughed and said, "I even have it myself…but Champ can live on for years with it, like I plan on doing. I have a topical cream that contains diclofenac sodium I will give you that may help with his pain and joint stiffness. After you get this swelling down, it's important to keep him active to stimulate circulation – just not too much. I'm sure you'll be able to gauge what's best for him."

Riley put his forehead against Champ's and scratched under the horse's chin. Slowly, Champ lowered the injured leg and put a little weight on it.

"Well, look at you.," Doc said encouragingly. "I've noticed you've always been a natural around animals. You're what we call a 'horse whisperer.' You have the right touch with animals and seem to know exactly what I would do for him."

The older man winked at Cal and said to Riley, "I could use you in my clinic on weekends and after school – that is if your mom's okay with it. I'm short-handed right now since my son's leaving for college after winter break."

Cal agreed wholeheartedly.

Riley thought for a moment, remembering Cal's words earlier about keeping busy, and then smiled for the first time. "I hope Mom agrees."

CHAPTER 41

IT WAS SNOWING OUTSIDE the window at Anthony's, a seafood restaurant in the Old Mill District of Bend. Hana and Micco watched the people either on cross-country skis or snowshoes pass along the trails near the edge of the Deschutes River that flowed north on its way to the Columbia River. On one wall near their booth was a black and white photo of two men using what looked like a long cross-cut saw to cut into the trunk of an old-growth Ponderosa Pine.

"I'm glad I finally asked you out," the petite Asian woman said. "I'm an impatient person and like to get things done."

Micco smiled. "I'm glad you did too. I wasn't sure if you were really interested in me – especially after that awkward kiss on New Year's."

"Awkward kiss?" she exclaimed. "I loved it!" Hana sighed. "And, I gave you so many clues, like always knowing exactly what you liked at the D&D."

A waiter came up and asked if they were ready to order.

Looking at the list of beverages, Hana said, "It's

Thursday and I don't have to go to work, so I'm in no hurry. I'd like a Cosmo, please." She closed the menu and looked at Micco. "We can order lunch later – after we finish our drinks."

When Micco nodded in agreement, he said, "I'll have a Black Butte Porter."

The waiter left and Hana sat back, smiling. "This is just like in that movie, Blind Date." She straightened the silverware on the table.

"I saw it, but I'm hoping our date doesn't end up like that one. It was pretty chaotic"

"I have over two hundred DVDs in my apartment, some VHS tapes, too."

"VHS is so old," Micco said.

She just smiled. "I have a machine that plays both versions. My mom is from South Korea and the American movies helped her to learn English."

"You were born here, right?"

"Yes. My dad was in the Army during the Korean War. That's when he met my mom and brought her here. It was like in Sayonara, but Mom was Korean, not Japanese. They were so in love."

"You sure know your movies."

"Besides that, I'm also a history buff. I love digging into the past"

Their drinks arrived and Hana took a small sip of her cocktail. "Yum, this is so much better than the ones I try to make at the D&D. It's a true art to get the right balance of champagne and juice." She looked over the rim of her glass and said, "So, tell me about yourself."

Micco sat back in his chair. "I grew up on the Jamison Ranch with Cal, near Terrebonne."

"So that's why you two are always together."

He nodded and continued. "My dad is the foreman

there, which is unheard of for a Northern Paiute, but Mr. Jamison believed in him and they were friends for years – until Cal's dad died."

Hana sipped her drink and waited.

"I joined the Marines with Cal right after high school graduation. But, unlike him, I went into the tech field. I've always loved computers – my first was a Commodore 64."

"Mine, too, and I still have it!" she exclaimed. "What a coincidence."

Micco continued sharing his background with Hana. After a while, the waiter came back and asked if they were ready to order food. The two looked at each other and ordered more drinks.

"Okay, it's your turn, Hana. What did you do after high school?"

"My dad always wanted me to go into some sort of Biology major. But, after my class with Cal in high school, which I hated, I chose differently. I studied at MIT—"

"Wait," Micco exclaimed. "You went to MIT? Even though we come from different cultures, we have the same interests. How did you end up as a waitress at the D&D?"

She looked out the window for a moment, then said, "My dad got sick, so I had to quit and come home. He died about a year later, so I stayed to help my mom. I've never had the chance to use the geek skills I learned."

The pair continued talking for over an hour. Then, Micco began to think of a plan and his face lit up.

"What?" Hana asked, wiping a cheek with her hand. "Do I have something on my face?"

He smiled and took her hand. "No, you're perfect. I think I know a way you can use those skills you learned at MIT."

Hana then said, "First, I think we should get something to eat. These mimosas are going to my head."

After they placed their order, she leaned in and asked, "So, what is this plan you talked about?"

"Cal is now working as a PI."

"That sounds exciting. Have you had any juicy cases yet?"

"We had one that was fairly easy to solve, but I really had fun setting up the surveillance equipment. It involved a possible ghost, which was so awesome."

Hana leaned in - her eyes wide with anticipation. "A ghost?"

"Well, the guy who hired us thought it was his dead brother's ghost causing the vandalism. But it turned out to be live people after all, and a couple of raccoons. Maybe if we get another case, you could come up to my place and help me set up the evidence board and work on info gathering for Cal."

"I'd love that! Count me in."

CHAPTER 42

MAJOR WALT MORRISON WAS in a secured room at the Camp Lejeune headquarters building with other Marine officers. Images of a bombed area in Afghanistan were visible behind one officer wearing desert fatigues on a large video display. Maps and papers spread before the uniformed men and women seated at the U-shaped table in the room.

"This attack was in the Helmand Province, near Sangin." Lieutenant Sanders reported on the screen as sounds of large vehicles drove by. "It was caused by a single explosive device while our troops were attempting to evacuate civilians. We lost several men."

Major Morrison said, "This is very similar to what happened to Cal Jamison's team the prior year."

"I agree, sir. A Marine Special Ops team was providing security for a local government. This time, it looks like the same type of device was used. But, during the commotion, there were several valuable gems stolen, Lapis Lazuli to be exact."

"These could help finance the Taliban's operation," a

woman officer in the room added.

The lieutenant paused a moment, then asked, "Sir, I think Jamison should be brought in for this."

The major looked at the other officers, then shook his head. "Cal just retired and he has family obligations now. I think we can handle this."

"I'm sorry to hear that," Sanders said.

"How soon can you get back here?" Major Morrison asked the lieutenant.

CHAPTER 43

IT WAS APRIL WHEN Cal parked his Jeep and trailer at the Ten-Mile Sno-Park near Paulina Lake. The roads had not been opened yet and snow was still on the ground and trees, but today was unseasonably warm for Spring. He'd brought extra clothes with outerwear, like the ones he'd used during his cold-weather missions as a Marine Raider, but today he figured he'd be peeling off some of the layers he'd worn before he was done fishing.

He unloaded the Double J's utility snowmobile that was sometimes used on the ranch and placed a small cooler and his fishing gear on it. It was a beautiful early morning before sunrise in the Newbury Volcanic area of the Deschutes National Forest. He never got tired of Central Oregon's rugged land and took a deep breath of the clear, crisp air.

As he drove toward the hot springs area on the northeastern side of the lake, Cal noticed how exhausted he was. Glenn had insisted he take a break and get some time alone, especially since it was the opening day of fishing season. *You haven't stopped since you got home*, his grandfather had said.

Cal had forgotten that Spring was the busiest time on a ranch with daily calving at all hours of the day, feeding orphaned calves, and moving herds to new pastures. The Kiger mares would not foal until the end of the season and Micco and his cousin, Tocho, were a big help. All three younger men let Glenn be in charge, but they did most of the work.

Coming up on the hot springs area, he stopped the vehicle quite a few feet back from the lake's shoreline and got off. Looking at the water, he was pleased that he'd been right. This area of the lake was generally the first to thaw and there were only a few large chunks of ice floating out away from the water's edge. There had been years when Paulina was ice free this same weekend.

The day before he came to the lake, he had stopped at the fly-fishing store in Sisters to get some new equipment. When Cal told Kevin, the owner, about going fishing for the large Brown trout at Paulina Lake, he'd suggested a Sage 9 1/2" six-weight rod with a Scientific Angler's slow-sinking "Emerger Tip" for fishing just under the surface, and a special sinking line for the deep ledges called a Sweeper that was a Type3/5/3 sink rate to really get the black leeches down past the abundant rocky drop offs found all around the lake just off shore. Cal walked to the back of the snowmobile and checked the ice in the cooler. He smiled as he remembered Glenn asking him to bring back some dinner.

As he took out the tackle box, Cal stopped as memories flooded back to him of times he and his dad fished together when he was young. This was his dad's box that Cal decided to start using when he was on medical leave. Fly fishing had been some of his therapy to get his right arm back in shape.

A Bald Eagle cried as it soared overhead, bringing Cal back to the present. Normally he preferred to fly fish in rivers and streams in warmer weather, but this was the season to have some fun stillwater fly fishing. He checked his other gear, stopped to put on his neoprene chest waders, and carried everything he'd need as he walked toward the water's edge.

From his work on the ranch, Cal had blisters and sore muscles, which reminded him of his Marine basic training. He realized how much he had missed life on the ranch. He really enjoyed riding his Kiger Mustang, Bravo, every day again, especially now that the weather was warming up. Sleeping under the stars and spending more time with grandparents and friends, he thought, *Life is good.*

The fishing was often best early in the morning. He chose the Black Marabou and Simi-Seal Leech that Kevin had suggested and tied it onto the heavy sweeper line. Cal's dad had a fishing mapbook that gave the location of the contours of each drop-off zone around the lake. Here the shoreline was a challenge to wade, but it put Cal in a spot where he could make a backcast away from the trees behind him on the shore, and out far enough to put his fly in front of hungry fish. He knew from his dad's charts that his fly was getting out to twenty-one feet of water, more than enough for a bid Brown trout to be hiding.

As he made the first cast with his fly rod, the sun was about to come up on the horizon. Sunrises over the Newberry Caldera were usually spectacular, but this morning there was an ominous feeling about it. The sky had a reddish glow and Cal remembered a friend in the Navy once saying, *Red sky in the morning, sailor take warning...* This made him remember the guy Hana had told him about who was looking for him. He wondered who that could've been.

He didn't get any takes from the fish, so he moved to another section of the shoreline. Looking at the insects in the area, he changed to the slow-sinking Emerger Tip line and an Olive & Black Bead head Assassin nymph and cast close to the bank in about thirty-five to forty feet of water.

Then, once he finished casting as his dad taught him, Cal kept the tip of his rod down toward the waterline so he could feel when a fish took the lure. He did the slow countdown to allow the fly to sink and start the retrieve to simulate the chironomid pattern. He knew that trout loved to follow the food, so he was very patient.

Cal had his first take. Holding the rod tip up, he pulled the line in to keep it taught as the fish fought on the other end. Finally, the fish surfaced and he saw that he'd caught a small Kokanee, a dwarf red salmon. He continued pulling until the fish tired, and then he used the long-handled net to snag the fish so he could unhook it. He gently held the now calm fish for a few seconds, then released it back into the water head first – a tradition his dad taught him, which Cal always believed came from Winnie.

As he continued to fish, with each repetitive cast of the line to get the fly to the perfect spot, Cal began to relax. His grandfather had been right - he did need this break. He thought of his most recent PI case. A sixty-year-old woman living in Ashland was searching for a long-lost friend from college. The guy was her first love. It didn't take long for Micco to look up the almanac for their college in Eugene, and he knew where to check next for possible family members and other associations. On one online media site, Micco found a recent link to the man in New York working as a book editor.

Being somewhat cautious with that case, Cal wondered what if the man didn't want to be found by this woman, so he made contact with him first and explained why he was looking for him after all these years. The guy was elated, saying he never forgot the woman. So, Cal gave him her information and hoped they'd found true happiness.

AFTER ABOUT AN HOUR, Cal had a few nice-sized Rainbow trout and a couple more Kokanee in his cooler on the back of the snowmobile.

He was about to stop fishing when he decided to change to a floating line and larger Black Beetle dry fly. After a few casts, using the double-hauling method to get more distance, his fly landed about thirty-five to forty feet out in the water. He'd been using a sort of stop-and-go retrieve that he'd read the Brown trout went after when suddenly, Cal hooked another.

"Wow, this is a really big one!" he exclaimed as he struggled, his pole bending almost in half from the weight of his catch. In May of 1993, the state record for Brown trout was set when one of those was caught at this lake weighing over twenty-seven pounds. He got excited as he slowly pulled in the line, releasing some to let the fish fight in hopes he didn't snap the leader…

Eventually, he saw what he'd snagged and almost dropped his fishing rod. Staggering back from the shore, he couldn't believe his eyes. Never in his wildest dreams did he ever expect this to happen. He'd caught a human body at the end of his line! Taking a deep breath, he slowly continued to pull the body to the shoreline.

Immediately, Cal pulled out his cellphone and prayed he'd find a signal. Walking back toward the snowmobile, he located one bar and quickly dialed Andy's mobile number.

THE MAN WATCHED JAMISON through binoculars

from a distant ridge, lying on his belly in the snow. He didn't think he'd ever be back to this area again, but felt it was fitting as he watched his target pull the body from the lake. It had been a long wait, but now he was back.

Knowing that official vehicles would be arriving soon, he decided to wait and have some fun, stalking Jamison for a bit longer.

CHAPTER 44

CAL KNEW HE NEEDED to leave the body as he found it for the medical examiner. He was glad he'd brought a thermos of hot coffee, which he sipped while he kept a vigilant watch since animals such as coyotes, cougars, and black bears had been sighted in the area. With the body lying at the water's edge, it was fair game.

After he'd called Andy, Cal went back to the body. It was hard to tell how long it had been in the somewhat icy water. It was face down, so he was unable to check for identification, but he could see that the skin was bloated. All kinds of scenarios went through Cal's mind as to how this person could've ended up in the lake since it was certain it had been there for a considerable amount of time.

Andy was the first to arrive as he drove up on a county snowmobile. Then, Cal heard the sound of a Sno-Cat engine approaching the lake and assumed it was the officials arriving. He was surprised to see that it was one from the LaPine substation of the County Sheriff's Department as it plowed a road for the other recovery vehicles. But then, that made sense - LaPine was closer than Bend.

Cal waved his friend over to where he stood. Andy stopped and dismounted from his vehicle.

"What the hell happened?" Andy asked as he grabbed the necessary equipment. "Your message was very cryptic."

"I was fly fishing and snagged a body," Cal replied, pulling his collar up around the back of his neck as he felt a chill down his back.

"For real? With a fly rod?"

"Yes, I was fishing for the large Brown trout. The body's over there."

Cal walked to the water's edge, the corpse lying face down near the bank. "It's exactly as I found it. Once I began to reel it in, thinking I'd caught a big fish, I stopped when I saw what it was."

The fishing hook was still attached to the back of the jacket of the victim. The clothes were like any other person in the northwest, but more for colder weather - a winter parka, plaid flannel shirt, and jeans.

As part of his job as a detective, Andy got busy taking photos and making sketches of the crime scene. "Never saw anything like this in my life," he said.

Another Sno-Cat arrived and Sheriff Scott Morrow was the first to dismount, leaving Deputy Rupert Bateman to get all the equipment. Cal had known the sheriff since he was a young teenager when he worked at the county while he was secretly looking for answers to his father's death.

The sheriff caught up with them and the three men stood and stared at the corpse.

"This is crazy," Morrow said.

"I've seen numerous dead bodies before," Cal said, "but this is new to me, as well." He cleared his throat and added, "Since I'm the one who caught it, sir, I'd like to be involved in this case. You know about my Private

Investigator's license, right?"

"Yes, I heard." Morrow stood with his hands on his hips and shrugged. "I'll just have to see."

Rupert came up carrying several silver cases. "Damn, it's a long way up here," he complained but stopped when he saw the body. He dropped the cases and said, "Whoa…now this is what I call a cold case."

No one laughed at the deputy's humor.

"Mind your manners," Cal snapped. He never really liked the deputy, but he wasn't sure why.

Just then, Cal was pleased to see Dr. Jordan Hansen, the county medical examiner, arrive with her assistant, Peter Edwards. The beautiful redhead was driving an all-wheel-drive county transport van with chains on the tires. Peter got out and went to the back to get a stretcher. Jordan walked to where the men stood, wearing thigh waders, and carrying her medical bag.

"You came prepared, Doc," Cal said, looking at her legs. They had worked together before on Luther's murder the prior fall, and, like him, she was a pilot.

"We had some prior info about the victim's location." She looked and Andy and asked, "You've taken photos of the victim?"

"Yes, ma'am."

Jordan first did a visual examination of the body. With gloved hands, she cut the fishing line and left the hook in the jacket. Peter waded in and helped her carefully turn the body over, which was still pretty stiff. The bare hands and face were very swollen and some skin was starting to separate from the bone.

"Oh, I'm going to barf," Rupert said.

"Not at my crime scene, mister!" Dr. Hansen ordered.

She then continued going over the body. "It will be difficult to identify this victim, but the lower right leg is missing, which means this is most likely an amputee." She looked at the sheriff and asked, "Was a prosthetic device found?"

Morrow stared at Andy, who then replied, "Not that I've seen."

She nodded and said, "You may need to order some divers, Sheriff, to see if a prosthesis can be located. There may be a number on it to ID the victim."

Sheriff Morrow looked at the LaPine supervisor who rode in on the first Sno-Cat. The man nodded. "I'll radio the DA," he said and walked back to his vehicle.

Cal looked down at the body, now seeing for the first time the way part of the right pant leg sunk below the surface. He was reminded of his friend, Angel, but quickly dismissed it. Too improbable, he thought.

The medical examiner turned to her assistant. "We'll need to get the body out of this water and to the hospital morgue as quickly as possible."

"On it, Doctor," Peter said. He told Rupert to put on some extra waders that he'd brought. When ready, the two men took the body that was still mostly frozen out of the water and into a body bag on the stretcher.

"Look at this, Doctor," Peter said as he held up a gray thermos that he'd found in the victim's coat pocket.

"That's probably why the body was so close to the surface," Jordan said as she placed the container into an evidence bag. "Considering the body's condition and the water's temperature, it would take longer for it to resurface unless there was something on it containing air."

Morrow then asked, "Any idea of a time of death, Doc?"

Jordan shook her head. "I'm sorry, but it's going to be very hard to tell that until the full autopsy. I do know this is a male and that the body was probably underwater for months, at least."

Then, the sheriff and examiner followed as the stretcher was carried to where the van was parked.

Cal and Andy remained near the water's edge, gathering his equipment.

BACK NEAR CAL'S SNOWMOBILE, as he was putting his gear away, he was telling Andy about his new business adventure. "I didn't get a chance to fill you in on my first PI case."

"No, what was it?"

"A simple report of vandalism, which I learned was not a crime, but a veteran trying to help an old man."

Cal stowed the last of his tackle and said, "Micco told me you decided not to take that State Police job." He looked at his friend and added, "I think that's a mistake."

"Maureen thinks so, too. We're still talking about it." Andy watched as the body was being taken away. "I think this case will be a lot harder to solve than your first one." He patted his buddy on the back and said, "I'm glad you're back."

Cal nodded. "Me, too. I don't think I ever mentioned a man on my team in the military. He and I were the only survivors of that blast in Afghanistan. On my flight home, I just missed him when I went to Nebraska."

"You were in Nebraska?" Jordan said behind Cal.

He turned, not realizing that she was within hearing distance. "Yes, uh, Red Cloud..." he said, but he didn't mention his side trip to Omaha.

CHAPTER 45

THE HOSPITAL MORGUE WAS cold and sterile, but it was where Jordan felt more alive. She always believed that she was destined to do this job, ever since the deaths of her parents. That was when she began studying forensic pathology.

Cal talking about Nebraska brought all her memories flooding back. She tried hard to push the horror of that day deep into the depths of her mind, but it was little things like this that easily brought them back to the surface.

"Damn him!" she exclaimed.

"I'm sure it wasn't his fault he died like this, Dr. Hansen," Peter said.

Jordan looked up in surprise. "No, I'm sorry," she said to her assistant, shaking her head. "I was thinking about something else."

She turned to the two young people standing next to the examination table where the body lay. Peter came to work for her the prior year. Aleshia was Jordan's young forensic photographer and had been there for two years.

"Aleshia," Jordan said, "please take detailed photos of

the body, and Peter, get full x-rays and log any abrasions."

"Yes, Dr. Hansen," Peter said.

"We need to work fast," the examiner cautioned. "After my preliminary exam, the cadaver will begin to decompose very quickly, so it is imperative that we get it sent to the Crime Lab in Clackamas as soon as possible. They'll be able to determine if the victim was dead before going into the lake."

The striking African-American woman used her digital Nikon SLR camera to take numerous images of the man at various angles that she could later download to her computer.

Jordan walked around the naked body on the table and added, "I wish we could take a blood sample but this body needs to be thawed to the core at the Crime Lab to get any fluids. I'm sure the reliability might still be questionable due to dilution from water exposure, depending on how long he was in the lake."

"Since there was no prosthetic device found at the scene of the crime, is there any indication that there could've been foul play?" Peter asked.

"I'm not sure yet. I now see that this man had a suspension socket, which means there would be no implanted part with a serial number to look up. We'll need full dental x-rays. I'll call the Forensic Dentist to ID the victim."

Aleshia said, "This is so sad. I wonder who this man was."

"I'm wondering why this popsicle was in a semi-frozen lake." Peter smiled but knew his morgue humor was sometimes lost on some people. "Maybe a suicide?"

"I think he was staying at the lodge and simply fell in," Aleshia offered.

Jordan smiled and shook her head. "Always the

optimist. I'm sure all will be revealed in due time."

While Aleshia and Peter worked, Jordan put on a headset and began dictating the conditions of the body into the microphone. "Decomposition, called adipocere, would progress very slowly in cold-water temperatures. The face is unrecognizable due to yellow-brown adipocere and skin sloughing…"

After Jordan was finished and the recorder stopped, Aleshia said, "I'm done. I'll go make copies for your report."

"Thank you," Jordan said as she removed her gloves.

She turned to her assistant. "It's time to send our body and all evidence to the Crime Lab in Clackamas."

"Will do, Doctor." Peter prepared the body to be transported.

Jordan looked at the evidence bag containing the thermos. "Also, ask that the Forensic Toxicologist tests the thermos for fluids first, which will give us quicker results than a blood sample. I hate waiting…"

A FEW MOMENTS LATER, Jordan was sitting at her desk, finishing her notes. She looked up as Andy and Cal entered the room. Cal stood to one side, letting Andy take the lead.

"Where's the body?" Andy asked.

"On its way to Clackamas. We only have a small window since it was still partially frozen." Jordan added, "I'm sorry gentlemen, but I don't have anything conclusive for you yet. I can't tell if he drowned or why he was in the lake in the middle of winter."

"Are there any marks or tattoos to identify him?" Cal asked.

"None that I can see just yet. It's hard to tell if external injuries could've caused his death."

Andy looked at his friend, knowing how this was troubling him since he was the one who discovered the body. "How long before we have the results of the autopsy?"

Jordan said, "I should have the Forensic Pathologist's preliminary report within forty-eight hours.

She looked at the two men she'd worked with on a prior case and saw the frustration on their faces. "I know, I hate it too. I'll call when I know more."

As Cal was about to leave, Jordan said, "I've finished the repairs on my Carbon Cub plane and have taken her up for a few test runs, so I know she is safe. Would you like to join me for a flight sometime?"

Cal smiled and said, "Absolutely. I'm free tomorrow and I could use the distraction while we wait for the autopsy report."

CHAPTER 46

A FEW DAYS LATER, Jordan taxied her red and silver airplane along the cleared small airstrip behind her house west of Bend. Within a very short while, she and Cal took off into the air.

"This is some aircraft," Cal said into his headset from the rear tandem seat as he looked around Jordan at the control panel. There were minimal gauges and an electronic engine monitor, no attitude indicator, just airspeed, VSI and altimeter.

Jordan turned her head and smiled from the front seat. "I love this plane; she does short take-offs and landings and is a lot of fun to fly."

He was surprised at how quickly they had ascended. The small Carbon Cub EX was a much simpler plane than Cal's Skyhawk, concise and streamlined. It had a fixed-pitch propeller and solo pilot flying from the front seat.

"What speed do you like to cruise at?" he asked.

"About 100-mile per hour," she said as they soared over the downtown Bend area. "She has a Titan 340cc 180 horsepower engine. This baby climbs like she's on fire.

She's my favorite because of a number of reasons, but mostly because I can pretty much take her just about anywhere. She lands at forty to forty-five feet, which is super slow and great in the mountains."

"You'll have to show me sometime, but maybe not today in the snow."

He'd done some research on this plane and found that they are homebuilt experimental aircraft. The kits are constructed in Yakima, Washington. He remembered that Jordan had told him she'd bought her plane already assembled.

Jordan pulled the stick to bank the plane left and said, "I thought we'd fly down toward Paulina Peak. Is that okay with you?"

Cal thought about the body he'd just found at the lake nearby, then said, "Why not."

As they flew south, they went over the High Desert Museum, one of Cal's favorite places. Then, on toward Sunriver, where Camp Abbot was built during WWII. Now, Sunriver was a large residential and resort area with an incredible observatory and nature center.

They turned east and the Newberry Volcano wilderness came into view with the lofty Paulina Peak in the distance. Jordan circled the plane around Oregon's largest lava creation as the sun glinted off the smooth black surface of the natural glass of the Obsidian Flow that was created thousands of years before.

"I never get tired of where I live," Cal said.

"Agreed. I call this part of Oregon the 'outback,' since it's so unique and diverse."

"Have you been to Frenchglen? It's a small town south of Burns near the Steens Mountain. That's true outback country. You could land this plane on the Alvord Desert there."

"No, I haven't, but it sounds intriguing."

Jordan banked again to fly over the East Lake, then on to Paulina Lake and the hot springs area.

She said, "I can't imagine what it was like to find a dead body on the end of your fishing line."

"Pretty unreal," was all Cal said.

As they circled the lake, Jordan said, "I've been thinking about outfitting the Cub with floats. They have little wheels so as to be amphibious. If the wheels are hidden in the floats, it lands on the water. Then you can flip a lever, the small wheels come out and you can land on a runway. Very versatile."

Cal nodded and smiled. "I can see you landing down there, after the thaw, of course, unless you get skis instead of floats."

"With skis, it's best to land on groomed snow, but not completely necessary."

Eventually, they circled Paulina Peak to the south. Cal looked around and could see all of the mountains in the distance between California and Washington. It was an incredible view.

ON THE FLIGHT BACK, the sun glinted off a golden band on Jordan's left wrist. Cal could tell it was made of Black Hills Gold. "Nice bracelet," he said.

She looked at it for a moment, then said, "My dad gave it to me after I graduated from Med school – just before I went to Hawaii."

"It's beautiful." Cal thought for a moment of what Kurt Stone told him when he was in Omaha. It was after she'd returned from that trip that she found her parents dead.

"Why were you in Nebraska?" she finally asked.

"A friend of mine from the military lives in Red Cloud. I was flying back home from the east coast and thought I'd stop in." He paused and decided to keep his stop in Omaha to himself for now. "I got snowed in overnight, then headed back to Oregon."

"Are you and Mary Creswell getting serious?" Jordan asked.

Cal frowned, confused by the quick change in subject, but then he sometimes used that tactic when he didn't want to talk about something.

"How do you know about Mary?"

"Bend isn't that big of a town."

"No, to answer your question. Surprisingly, I think my brother, Jack, is more interested now, so I'm taking a step back." He really didn't want to get into the 'friends only' thing with Jordan.

"What about you?" he asked, figuring that was fair play.

She shook her head. "My work right now takes up most of my time."

"I understand," Cal said.

Jordan looked at the western horizon where the sun was getting lower in the sky. "A few years ago, I dated a guy during my Fellowship in Arizona, where I studied Forensics…It was too late when I learned he was not a nice man."

Cal didn't respond but filed this new information away in his mind.

They flew in silence for a while then Jordan said, "I know nothing about fishing. What's it like to fly fish?"

"Nothing like it. My dad taught me how to use a fly rod. It's magical if you're using a dry fly. You can see the fish coming to the surface to grab your lure." He looked at the back of Jordan's ginger-colored hair and added, "I'll teach you someday."

CHAPTER 47

WHEN CAL WALKED INTO the sheriff's office in Bend, he was glad Andy was alone. He was surprised to see his friend going through a bag of clothes.

"Hey, Cal," Andy said, smiling. "I was about to call you when this came in. Sheriff has agreed to bring you on as a consultant on the floating man case."

"Awesome. What's all this?" Cal asked, pointing to the bag.

"We located another abandoned SUV. This one was behind a dilapidated barn at old man McDonald's farm. Everyone knows he always closes the place up and goes to New Mexico for the winter. He just called us when he found the vehicle after he got home. I was surprised to see this stuff was left behind."

"What do you mean 'another' SUV?"

Andy stopped and took a deep breath. "Oh, I guess I need to bring you up to speed on what we know so far." He told Cal about the first vehicle found at Ten-Mile Sno-Park. "It was registered to Darren Lions and the sheriff thinks there may be a connection to our case. They're bringing him in now for questioning."

"Got any information on this guy?"

"He's Army Reserves and works for Les Schwab tire company. I talked to this guy and there's something about him I don't like."

"Was this stuff from Lions' vehicle?" Cal asked.

"No, this was from the vehicle we found at McDonald's. We'd been looking for it since the rental company reported it missing last January."

Cal watched as Andy resumed searching the bag from the recent vehicle. When he pulled out a black fleece vest with the nested 'V' logo of Vail Ski Resort on it, Cal said, "I know a guy who has a vest like—"

Andy continued, "The second vehicle this came from had a rental agreement for a guy from Nebraska."

Cal sank down on a chair next to Andy's desk and stared at the ski pin under the Vail logo. He took a deep breath and said, "Let me guess. Was it Angel Ramirez from Red Cloud?"

Andy stopped and stared at Cal. "How the hell would you know that? That name was in the Paulina Lake registration book, too – the guy who never checked out."

Cal swallowed hard. "I think the body I snagged was Angel, the man I told you about that was on my team in the Middle East." Nodding to the vest, he added, "Angel grew up in Silverthorne, Colorado and spent every spare moment skiing the black diamond runs in Vail, and I was with him when he got that ski pin years ago in July. We skied Palmer Glacier on Mt. Hood just before we were about to be deployed. Angel liked boasting that he skied there on his birthday. We had to quit by noon because the snow was getting slushy." He stopped and look at Andy, "I guess we might possibly know who the victim was."

"I'll alert the ME to check those areas for dental

records."

The only sound now in the room was the motor of a refrigerator in the break room kicking on.

CHAPTER 48

WHILE ANDY WENT TO make a fresh pot of coffee, Cal took advantage of being alone in the squad room of the Sheriff's Office. He went to the evidence board and scanned the photos and reports they had so far on the body found in the lake. Even though the post-mortem report had not come in yet to determine the identity of the victim, Cal felt in his gut that this was Angel, his friend and comrade.

He quickly began jotting notes about the evidence on the back of a receipt he had. He turned the receipt over and realized it was for the new fishing line and fly he'd recently purchased at the fishing store in Sisters. The owner, Kevin, had suggested them when Cal told him about going fishing for the large Brown trout at Paulina Lake.

Taking a deep breath, he looked again at the evidence. Darren Lions was in the Army Reserves and had done one tour in Afghanistan. He also was a bit of a hothead, always getting into trouble around town. The rental agreement with Angel's name on it for a Nissan Xterra was dated the same day that Cal had arrived in Red Cloud, Nebraska.

There were too many coincidences now between the body and Angel, and over the years, Cal had learned to treat all coincidences as suspicious.

Andy returned with two mugs of steaming coffee and sat at his desk. "I know the sheriff said you can consult on this case, but not sure he'd want you going over our evidence."

"I'm just trying to catch up," Cal said as he put the receipt in a pocket.

THE DOOR OPENED AND Cal quickly sat down next to Andy's desk. Sheriff Morrow and Rupert arrived escorting a thirty-something, dark-haired man. He wasn't in handcuffs, but he didn't seem happy to be there.

"Awe, dammit, Jamison," Rupert yelled. "What the hell are you doing here again?"

Cal never liked Rupert Bateman, but he just ignored the deputy's rantings because he and the sheriff got along pretty well.

"Take Mr. Lions to the Interview Room," Morrow told Rupert.

"I'll answer any questions you have, but like I told you, I didn't do anything," the young man said as he was led from the room.

"What are you doing here, Cal?" Morrow asked as he removed his hat and gun belt and placed them on his desk.

Andy stepped in and said, "I asked him here, sir," he lied. "Cal thinks he knows who the victim is."

Morrow turned and stared at Cal. "You know the victim? He hasn't even been ID'd yet."

"Maybe," Cal replied. "Based on something we just found, Angel Ramirez was one of the men on my team in the Marines."

Morrow looked at Andy.

"Ramirez was the name on the rental form for the SUV we found this bag in," the detective said.

The sheriff sat down and shook his head. "How do you always seem to be mixed up in my cases, Jamison?"

Cal shrugged and said, "Just lucky, I guess, sir."

"Tell me what you know about this man, Ramirez," Morrow said and took notes as Cal filled him in.

"I hope this won't be a conflict of interest," Cal said.

After he was finished, all three men looked up as the front door to the office banged open.

"Where the hell is my son?" a large, older man roared.

Morrow stood and held up his hands. "Calm down, Mr. Lions, he's just here to help us in our investigation. He hasn't been accused of any crime."

The sheriff turned to Andy and said, "Would you please take Pete to the waiting area and see if he wants anything to drink while he waits."

"I don't want to sit in some waiting room!" the young man's father yelled. "I want to see my son."

"He is not a juvenile, sir," Morrow said, then added, "We just want to ask him a few questions."

The sheriff looked at Andy, who saw the look on the sheriff's face and knew he was to stay with the dad until Rupert came out.

As Pete Lions and Andy left the squad room, Morrow turned to Cal. "Do you know Darren Lions?"

Cal shook his head. Not wanting to get Andy in any trouble, he also fibbed a little. "Never heard of him. How's he connected to this case?"

"He owns the SUV found up at Paulina Lake."

"Can I watch your questioning?"

The sheriff thought for a few seconds and agreed.

LATER, ANDY JOINED CAL in the observation room.

"You hardly ever talk about that event in Afghanistan," Andy said.

"I know and I apologize." He paused for a moment, then said, "If this body turns out to be my friend, I'd like to take Angel's things to his family when they can be released."

Andy nodded. "I think I can arrange that."

"He used to have so many ski badges pinned to his parka from every mountain he ever skied on, they looked like all the medals on his military uniform."

Cal watched through the two-way glass as Morrow walked into the room where Darren sat at the table. A small red light flashed on a camera hung in one corner of the room indicating the incident was being taped.

"For the record," Morrow began, "your name is Darren Lions and you live on…" Morrow asked numerous mundane questions about the suspect's life.

The young man looked nervous but nodded to the questions.

"I need you to answer my questions for the record," Morrow said.

"Yes, to everything you just asked me."

"What were you doing up at Paulina Lake around January 2nd of this year?"

Darren looked confused. "I was never up there. Like I told your detective at my house, I drive the Schwab delivery truck. My last stop was in LaPine and when I got back to the Redmond airport, my car was gone."

Morrow looked at some papers in a file he'd brought in. Then, he asked some of the same questions Andy had used at the Lions' house to also put Darren's answers on tape, as well.

After about ten minutes, Morrow asked, "Where was your military duty?"

The suspect shifted in his seat, then said, "I'm stationed with the Army National Guard here in Bend and was sent to Afghanistan a couple of years ago. I was only there for three months. Then, I was called back again and returned after the holidays. My dad was pissed I had to miss everything."

"Do you know a man by the name of Angel Ramirez?"

Darren shook his head. "Nope." He quickly sat up and asked, "Is that the guy found at the lake that was recently on the news?"

"We do not know as yet," Morrow said, placing a photo of the victim on the table.

The young man turned away at the gruesome image. "Whoa, who the hell is that?"

"We're waiting for confirmation, but there is evidence that this may be Ramirez. He was staying at Paulina Lake, and then he and his vehicle disappeared. We just located that vehicle… Do you want me to believe that your SUV just magically ended up at the same location where this man was possibly killed?"

"Murdered?" Lions said, standing up. "But, I don't know anything about this!"

"Sit down," the sheriff said calmly. "We're still waiting for the post-mortem report, so we're not making any assumptions. We're just making sure all areas of our investigation have been sufficiently covered."

Sheriff Morrow looked up at the mirrored glass, knowing that he only had circumstantial evidence so far, then stood up.

"At this time, Mr. Lions, you are free to go. But, don't leave the area."

CHAPTER 49

CAL LEFT BEND AND drove toward the Double J Ranch, thinking about all the events that happened earlier that day. If this body was Angel, what the hell was he doing up at Paulina Lake? Was he the guy that was asking about him earlier at the D&D?

No answers came as he turned his Jeep off Route 20 and onto the Tumalo Reservoir Road after he passed the sign to the Tumalo State Park. He was so deep in thought he didn't see the vehicle tailing him.

The last time Cal saw Angel alive was after the attack in Afghanistan, when they both were taken on a Chinook helicopter to Camp Bastion, the nearest military medical facility. On arrival, they were separated for treatment. As Cal was being sent home for physical therapy and recovery, he'd learned that Angel went to Bethesda for his prosthetic device and training.

After a few months, when Cal heard that Angel had returned to Colorado, he went to visit him. But Angel's family told him that he'd gone to some remote cabin up in the mountains and refused to see anyone. They said he was spiraling into a deep depression and isolated himself away from the people who loved him. Refusing to be pushed aside like the others, Cal went in search, but he and Angel had the same training and Angel knew how to disappear.

As Cal pulled into the lane to the Double J, he shook his head. He felt the sheriff was too quick to consider Darren Lions as a suspect, but at this time, he was the only link to Angel.

This seems too damned easy, he thought.

Cal was surprised to see Hana's red Hyundai parked outside of the garage. He stopped his Jeep next to her car and went up to Micco's to tell him about the possibility of the body being Angel's and to share what evidence he'd gathered so far.

THE OLD MAN PARKED the tan Impala he'd stolen from a shopping mall in Bend in a grove of nearby trees. The color of the vehicle blended into the landscape nicely, as he'd anticipated. He'd hated that he'd been pulled from his mission, but he had to follow orders.

After he killed Ramirez, he'd been called back to Afghanistan to work on another job that meant a lot to his regime and he was the best man for the job. The stash of those precious gems was known to only a few Afghans and he knew the family…

Now, taking out his binoculars, he looked around at the log house and other buildings. He smiled as his next target walked up the stairs to an apartment above the large garage.

"Now I know where Cal Jamison lives!" he said out loud.

CHAPTER 50

MRS. WILSON, A WIDOWER, brought her small Bichon Frise dog into the veterinarian clinic to be neutered. The dog and the woman wore matching red knitted sweaters.

"This nice young man is going to take excellent care of you, Mason," the woman said. She hugged and kissed the little white dog, who licked her face. Then she handed him to Riley.

"He's in good hands with Doc Thompson," Riley said. "We'll call you when you can pick Mason up."

"Is Doc in?" the woman asked hopefully.

"I'm sorry, ma'am, but he's out on a call."

After Mrs. Wilson left, he turned and took the little dog to the back room.

The young man looked into the dog's black eyes and said, "You have a life-changing event coming, my friend. I'm so sorry." Then, Riley put the fluffy animal into a cage.

He scratched the dog behind the ears and closed the door. He knew that Doc mostly worked on large animals, but the older man had a soft spot for this lady. Riley was so glad that Doc had arranged with his mom to lift his grounding if he agreed to work at the clinic. It was turning out to be good pay and he loved the experience.

JUST THEN, DOC CAME running into the clinic from the back, grabbed his bag, and said, "We have to go. There's been an accident at the ranch next door – Goldie's caught in a barbed-wire fence."

The two ran out and heard the shrieks of an injured animal. At a fence separating the two properties, Riley saw the panicked Palomino mare fighting to get free from the wire entwined around her front legs that was cutting into the flesh. As Doc went to help Mr. Blake to get the horse to lie down, Riley gently approached the animal's head and talked softly to her.

"Good girl," he kept repeating as he stroked the horse's dun-colored neck, covering the animal's eyes with one hand to block out what was going on around her. "Quiet Goldie. You'll be okay."

Eventually, the animal started to calm and lay there as Riley stroked her face and neck. When he saw the owner approaching with wire cutters, he again covered the animal's eyes and talked to her in his soothing voice he'd heard his dad use whenever one of their horses at home became frightened.

Once the mare was free from the wire, Doc examined her legs and chest.

"I'll need to sedate and treat her."

It took almost an hour to get the animal back into her stall in the neighbor's barn, bandaged and sedated.

"I thought you already replaced all that barbed wire with a smooth wire," Doc said to Mr. Blake.

"I've been meaning to do it but just never seemed to have enough time."

"I could maybe help," Riley said, "if it's okay with my mom."

Blake then said, "I'd appreciate that."

AS DOC AND RILEY walked back to the clinic, Doc said, "You were amazing with her, son."

Riley asked, "How did that happen?"

"Something probably frightened her and she ran into a fence. Unfortunately, Goldie's a horse that gets easily spooked. One year we found her three miles away because of some random fireworks."

"I was glad I could help keep her calm. My dad taught me how to do that."

"Luther was a good man." Doc looked at Riley. "You know, I think you could be able to do more. If you're there helping Blake with his fence, maybe you could spend some extra time with Goldie to be less nervous."

"I'll do some research and see what I can find."

Doc put his arm around Riley's shoulder. "How is your mom doing?"

"She's finished with her radiation treatment. I'm so glad Bonnie came to stay with us. She does most of my chores for me – which frees me up to come here."

"Your mom told me you're going to U of O after you graduate. Have you ever considered Veterinary School after college?"

Riley thought for a moment. "No, but I think I might like it."

"Let me give you a list of classes you should consider for Advance Placement during your last year in high school. Also, there are certain elective courses you'll need in college," Doc said as they entered the clinic.

"That'd be great," Riley said excitedly, starting to finally see a direction for his future.

"Also, you might want to consider Oregon State instead. They have a great Veterinary School in Corvallis."

Just then, the little dog in the cage started barking.

"Is that Mason I hear?" Doc asked.

"Yes, Mrs. Wilson brought him in earlier." Riley smiled as he looked at the older man. "She was really sorry she missed you."

CHAPTER 51

CAL MET ANDY IN the parking lot of the sheriff's office. Earlier, his friend had called him and said he needed to be there by ten o'clock that morning but didn't say why.

"So, buddy," Cal said, "what's up?"

"I've decided to take that State Police job in Salem. Maureen convinced me that we can live anywhere, which means more money for our kids' college educations."

"That's good to hear, but you could've told me that on the phone. It's calving season and I keep trying to put Glenn in charge of all the paperwork." He looked at his friend. "You'll be a great addition to their detective department, but you'll be missed around here."

Andy laughed, "I'm not so sure Rupert will miss me."

Smiling, Cal said, "We'll stay in touch for sure – you might be able to help me on some of my future cases."

As they walked toward the front door, Andy said solemnly, "Through dental records and your help, the ME was able to confirm the body you snagged was Angel's."

"I still can't believe he's dead. As soon as I thought it was him, I called my CO at Camp Lejeune." He glanced at

Andy and said, "I thought you had a good candidate for Angel's murder."

Andy nodded. "So did I. On a hunch, after we questioned Lions, I took a copy of his DMV photo to Paulina Lake Lodge. The bartender there was pretty sure that he'd seen him during the day on New Year's Eve. He said he never forgets a face. The district attorney charged Lions as a suspect in this case and we have him in custody."

"That's helpful, but is it enough to convict him?" Cal asked.

"Not according to the DA. He wants us to keep looking for more evidence to link Lions to the victim. Sheriff sent Rupert out to search the victim's SUV again."

They both stopped when they saw Dr. Jordan Hansen pull into the lot and park her car next to Cal's Jeep. He went over and held open the door of the vintage Chevy Blazer for her.

"Good morning, Dr. Hansen," Cal said smiling. "Nice car. What're you doing here?"

"I have the full Postmortem report." She placed her hand on his arm and added, "I'm glad you're here, and I'm so sorry about your friend."

The three walked somberly into the station.

AS THEY ENTERED THE squad room, Deputy Bateman looked up.

"Hell, Jamison," Rupert whined from his desk, "I hoped we were done with you."

"Not a chance," Cal said.

Just then, Sheriff Scott Morrow came out of the back room with Pete Lions.

"I'm going to that judge to see if I can't get him to set

bail for my son," Lions insisted.

"You do that, Pete," Morrow said. He turned to his deputy. "Rupert, will you please escort Mr. Lions from the premises."

"What was that all about?" Jordan asked.

"He's the dad of our suspect for the murder of Angel Ramirez," Morrow said. "What're you doing here, Doc? We're kind of busy right now."

She held out a file to him. "I've brought copies of the Crime Lab's final autopsy reports. Normally, I'd fax these over, but I wanted to make sure you saw this, Scott."

Morrow took the papers from her; Cal and Andy went to look over his shoulders.

Jordan said, "The victim's body showed no bruises, cuts, or broken bones - no signs of a pre-mortem struggle. At first, it looked like he simply died from drowning, but there was no pulmonary edema - water in the lungs."

Cal looked up and said, "He was dead before he went into the water?"

She nodded. "I'm afraid so. After the body was completely thawed, a toxicological analysis of the victim's blood was ordered. But that can take months to get the results back. In the meantime, the thermos bottle found in the victim's coat pocket was tested by the Forensic Toxicologist. I was then able to direct the Pathologist that there was a strong suspicion of poisoning and exactly what to look for in a blood sample. The lab tests were rushed to assist with the homicide investigation."

"And?" Sheriff Morrow asked, handing the papers to Andy.

Jordan looked at Cal. "I'm afraid your friend was poisoned."

"That explains it," Cal said, shaking his head. "Angel's a Marine, he wouldn't go down without a fight."

Andy said, "The lab report shows the poison was a combination of two plants: Datura extract and Rosary peas."

She nodded and explained. "Yes, I did some research. The Datura plant, also known as 'Jimson Weed,' is found in the U.S. It appears that the raw seeds are most deadly and could be extracted from the spiny pods, sometimes called 'Thornapples,' if they are mashed and strained to add the juice to a small amount of alcohol."

"How long before death once the poison was ingested?" the sheriff asked.

Jordan took a deep breath and said, "The fact is that blending Datura with Rosary peas causes pre-mortem symptoms – first is a GI irritation followed by rapid heart rate, confusion, hallucinations, and severe thirst with dilated pupils."

She stopped and looked at Cal and then added, "The victim died of heart failure after about four to six hours of taking the poison."

"Damn," Andy exclaimed. "This was a crime of passion."

Cal remained silent.

Jordan nodded. "Yes. The Rosary peas contain a poison called Albin that can be crushed and made into a paste and then liquified…"

Andy held up a sheet of paper and said, "Here's a photo of those plants."

Seeing one of the pictures, Cal said, "I've seen this Rosary plant before in Afghanistan."

Jordan nodded, "It is found in Africa and Afghanistan."

The sheriff said, "Now, there's another connection I was hoping for."

Just then, Deputy Bateman ran in with a sealed

evidence bag. "You're never going to guess what I found under the driver's seat in that other SUV," he said excitedly. "A pocket knife with Lions' name on it!"

Morrow pounded his fist on the counter. "By god, I think we've got our man for murder."

CHAPTER 52

A COUPLE OF DAYS later, before dawn, Cal and Micco were pulling bales of hay from the loft of the Double J barn to a trailer connected to a tractor. The cattle and horse herds were now in different pastures, but some of the grasses were still young and the air was chilly from a prior cold snap the night before.

"We need to get these out to the animals," Cal said, rubbing his right shoulder. His scars and muscles sometimes became sore when he did manual labor – a constant reminder of his injury.

Micco stopped and wiped his brow with a handkerchief. "And I'll make sure to check the water troughs."

Odie, Glenn's Australian Shepherd, came into the barn with his entire body wriggling with joy.

"Glenn must be up," Cal said. "I want to get this done before he comes out, so let's get moving."

"Your grandfather's been sick this whole month, which took quite a bit out of him. Winnie is helping us to keep him busy a little longer with the birthing and health records."

Cal laughed. "A little flu bug never kept that man down very long."

"He's not getting any younger, though." When Micco looked at his friend, he added, "You know you made the right decision, not re-enlisting."

"Yeah," Cal said, tossing the last bale onto the trailer. Just then, he heard their neighbor's dogs barking in the distance. "I wonder what's gotten into Gabe's pups this early. He's talked about starting a breeding program."

Micco shrugged and leaned against a stack of bales. Cal had noticed that his friend would sometimes get lost in his own thoughts. "What's up with you these days?" he asked.

"Isn't Hana uber smart?" Micco asked. "She was able to find the poison that killed Angel was also found in the same region in Afghanistan where you and your team were assigned. What a coincidence, huh?"

Cal shook his head. "You know how I feel about that. And I'm still not sure about Darren Lions being Angel's killer - just because he was in Afghanistan."

A horse in the barn whinnied and Cal removed his gloves as he walked over to his Kiger stallion in one of the stalls. He scratched the animal's forehead and ran his other hand down the long neck.

"Hey, Bravo," Cal said, "I know you need a ride, but that'll have to wait for a bit."

As Micco climbed down from the loft, Odie began to bark. He and Cal went to the large open door of the barn and watched as Andy drove up. The detective waved at the two men in the barn, then got out of the squad car. He pulled a small box from the back seat and walked to join them.

"You never get up before sunrise," Cal said to Andy. "And what're you doing driving a marked county vehicle?"

"I couldn't sleep and my car's in the shop." He set the box on a bale and said to Cal, "Did you know there's an old man in town asking questions about you?"

"That's interesting. When I was in Nebraska, a guy told me about an older man passing through Angel's hometown asking about him."

"Coincidence?" Micco said smiling.

Andy looked at his friends, not getting the joke.

"What's in the box?" Cal asked.

"Late last night, the DA released some of Angel's things not pertinent for the trial. I wanted to get them to you so you could return them to his family."

Cal opened the lid. The fleece vest was on top. He picked it up and said, "Angel loved to ski - before he lost his leg."

As he removed the item from the box, he felt something in an inside pocket and pulled out a piece of paper. He opened it and exclaimed, "Oh my god!"

The other two men moved in closer to see what was written on the paper.

"Is that a coded message?" Micco asked excitedly. "What's it doing in Angel's vest?"

"What does this mean?" Andy asked, trying to read the message over Cal's shoulder.

Cal explained. "As a kid, I always liked solving puzzles and cryptograms. When my team was developed, I created a code system that we could use for classified messages between each other. That way, if the notes got into the wrong hands, only we knew what it said." He stopped for a moment, then added, "It's been a long time since we used them."

"Let's take it upstairs to my place," Micco said as he took off his work gloves. "I could use some coffee, then we can feed the herd."

THE THREE MEN WENT to the apartment over the garage. Micco ran up first and immediately turned the whiteboard around to hide the notes that he and Hana had collected about Angel's case. Then, he went to the kitchen and poured three mugs of hot coffee.

"What's the cipher?" Micco asked.

Cal sat down. "First, I always chose a number as the key. Then, using the letters of the alphabet, you count that number and write down the corresponding letter."

"That was used by Caesar," Andy commented.

"Yes, try the number six," Cal said.

"So, if we use every sixth letter, we can maybe come up with the answer?" Micco asked as he sat at the counter.

"Why didn't we use something like this in high school?" Andy asked.

Cal smiled. "We had our own secret signals on the football field."

The three men worked together to decipher the message, while Cal solved it on his own in his head. He didn't disclose the true meaning of what Angel had written. The final words of the message said, "Semper Fidelis." Cal now knew who the assassin was - and he wanted to be the one to find him.

After a few moments, Micco said in frustration, "This doesn't make any sense."

Cal shook his head. "Maybe Angel's mind was being controlled by his PTSD hallucinations more than I thought."

Andy frowned at Cal. Then, he shrugged and said, "You knew Angel best. And, Sheriff Morrow believes he's got his man."

"Well, I still think that Morrow is wrong…" Cal walked

to the large whiteboard and turned it around.

Andy went over and started going over the evidence. "Who did all of this?" he asked.

"We did," Micco said, not mentioning Hana's involvement.

Andy turned and looked at Cal. "You know that if someone else killed Angel, you could also be in danger."

Cal simply shrugged his shoulders. "I still have three questions: Why would Lions leave his vehicle at the Sno-Park? If Lions was the killer, why did he take Angel's vehicle to McDonald's farm? And, how did he get home?"

"That's four questions," Micco said.

"Dammit, Cal," Andy said, "I thought we had this case solved. With McDonald's farm in the same area as Lions' home, I figured he could've walked."

"Maybe Lions was being framed by someone else," Cal suggested.

Andy chimed in. "That's possible, but who would do that?"

Cal shook his head to move things along. "I don't think we're going to solve anything today. We've got feed to get to our animals and, Andy, it's probably time you need to get to work."

CHAPTER 53

THE MAN WATCHED AS the sheriff's vehicle was still parked near the red barn. The plain clothesman was probably a detective. The man had been watching the nearby property for days now, hoping to get a chance to finally finish the job he was assigned to do over a year ago.

He looked around his surroundings at the grove of trees that hid the car he'd stolen in town. Dogs barked when he'd arrived, but thankfully they were quiet now.

Laying on a cold ridge, he tried to ignore the ache in his body and peered through the powerful binoculars at the ranch in the distance. As he did on every job, he surveyed the area. Black and white cattle stood in a pasture to the west of the red barn and a small herd of horses grazed by some Aspen trees. He saw a little old woman, wrapped in a heavy coat, come out of the log home.

An image of his own mother flashed in his mind. He seldom allowed himself to dwell on the past, but it had been a very long time since he'd seen her. When he was only ten, his father moved their family to Adana, Turkey. He'd hated it there and was angry at being taken away from his homeland and his friends, so he'd started acting out, getting into the wrong crowd of boys. That's why he'd been sent away to America.

The man thought of Darren Lions and smiled. He'd wanted to meet Lions face-to-face to tell him how he'd framed him for Ramirez's murder but felt justified that Lions would go to jail for it. He touched the mask on the side of his face where his scar was covered. It was a reminder of the year when he was a teenager, living with the Lions family. That's why the man knew his way around this area. Darren had struck him with his dad's golf club. He knew it was an accident, but he'd hated how the kids at that school used to call him 'Scarface.'

He and Darren looked so much alike that everyone thought they were twins. He'd decided to use that to his advantage at the lake lodge when he knew that Ramirez and that girl would be away for the day. He'd used Ramirez's cabin to remove his disguise and simply walk around the area, making sure he was seen. He'd even gone into the bar and ordered the same craft beer he knew Lions drank when they were teens.– "Pete's Wicked Ale." He even made a big fuss about it being discontinued in hopes that the bartender would remember him.

In his mind, the man now planned different ways to get to Jamison. He'd used poison before and he wasn't a trained sniper. He was better with bombs. But this time it was personal. He was in so much trouble with his handler because he had taken too long to finish this mission.

He became excited when he saw his mark come out of the space above the garage with the plain clothesman. He waited until the sheriff's vehicle drove away.

Jamison now stood outside the barn looking around, his hands on his hips. That was a familiar stance… Suddenly, the man stepped back farther under the trees.

When Jamison had turned his head his way, the man could swear his victim was looking right at him.

CHAPTER 54

AFTER ANDY LEFT, CAL looked up at the sky as it began to rain. He zipped up his jacket and rolled his right arm to relieve the tension. Like his grandfather, he hated to feel weak.

Cal smiled when he saw his grandmother come out of the house with her basket. She was wrapped up in her long wool coat and was going to feed her chickens and gather eggs for the day.

"Good morning, Winnie," he said. "How's Glenn today?"

"Ornery as ever," she said laughing. "He says that he's coming out soon to help you boys."

"Tell him we've got the animals taken care of and that I'll be in in a minute for some coffee."

Winnie nodded and went into the coop.

Cal knew that Glenn's health was not good and they had talked the night before over a bottle of fine Scotch about making a few changes at the ranch. They'd also discussed how Jack's new business adventure at the Jamison Ranch had already altered the old homestead., but now they understood the reason behind it all.

Andy's words came back to him and Cal knew they were true – he could be in danger. But that also meant that the people around him were, too. If any trouble came to his family and friends because of something he did or could have avoided, he would never forgive himself.

Just then, the hair on the back of Cal's neck stood up. It was a feeling that he'd learned on his job to never ignore. Slowly, his eyes surveyed the land around him until he saw the faint glint of sunlight on a vehicle parked in a grove of trees at the edge of Gabe's property. He stared for a long while – knowing that are was an unusual place to park a car.

In the Marines, MARSOC taught him to never ignore the atypical – each phase of training conditioned him to constantly be aware of his surroundings, no matter what circumstance he may find himself in during special operations. This feeling he had now put him on alert as if he was in one of those situations.

Winnie came out of the chicken coop and went back into the house.

Calmly, Cal took out his keys as he walked to his Jeep. He backed out and drove up the lane, then turned right onto the road that led away from the ranch. In a little bit, he smiled when he saw he was being tailed.

CHAPTER 55

CAL DROVE ALONG ROUTE 20 toward Sisters, figuring that the long line of traffic would delay an attack until he reached his destination. It was a Sunday when most vacationers started returning home after a weekend in Central Oregon. Looking into his rearview mirror, he saw the same tan Chevy was now a few cars behind him.

Before Plainview, he turned left onto the back roads that he knew would lead to the Whychus Creek trailhead, a fairly remote area this time of year. On the horizon stood the snow-covered Three Sisters and Broken Top mountains.

He looked back and smiled again. Cal prayed that the trail area would be vacant, leaving him alone to deal with whoever was following him.

He parked his Jeep and watched as the tan vehicle turned onto Three Creek Road. He knew he only had a few minutes, so he tore a piece of his red jacket and placed it onto a branch leading to the North Trail. Then, he ran to a place near the creek to hide and wait. Cal wished he'd brought a weapon, but as a trained Marine Raider, he was a weapon.

Assuming his assailant would be out of his element in the wooded area, Cal used that to his advantage. The soft sound of the creek trickled behind him and he saw a single white-tail deer walk down to the water's edge – a moment of serenity before all hell broke loose.

Cal heard footsteps on the gravel trail, which is the reason he'd chosen his position. The deer ran away and he saw the face and clothes of a much older man through the dense canopy. Cal wondered if this was the 'old man' Andy had talked about, yet his movements were that of someone much younger.

As the man came closer, Cal turned on a recording app on his cell phone and zipped it into a coat pocket. Then, he threw a rock to his right, which lured his attacker closer to his location. He could then see that the man was possibly wearing a prosthetic mask. Now, more than ever, Cal was certain that this had to be the man whose name Angel had written in his coded message.

Cal waited until the man passed him and then he stepped out onto the trail. "You looking for me, Badih Gaba?" he said calmly, trying to stall for time.

The man turned. "You are the last man on my list. I was the one who placed the bomb near the school that killed all the others on your team in Sangin – Cravens, Simon, and Marshall. Poisoning Ramirez here was the most fun. Now, Cal Jamison, your death will finally fulfill my mission!"

"But, why attack my team?" Cal asked, hoping to get all the information on tape.

"You were involved in the death of one of our leaders. It was personal for me because it occurred in the village I grew up in as a boy. Now it is your turn to die—"

Badih rushed at Cal, who deflected him with a turning

maneuver. Cal could see the rage in the man's eyes and he switched to an offensive tactic, using his MCMAP training. Martial Arts had saved his life numerous times before in hand-to-hand combat, but this man pulled a knife and came at him again.

In the struggle, Cal's fingers caught hold of the edge of the mask, which came off, revealing the scarred cheek he'd seen before in the Helmand Province of Afghanistan.

"It's your turn to die," Badih yelled and again lunged. Cal grabbed Badih's wrist and twisted, causing the man to drop the knife. As the two men fought, their feet came near the edge of the creek bank. Badih punched Cal on his right shoulder, causing a stabbing pain to shoot down his back. Cal arched back, bumping his head against his assailant.

At that moment, Badih screamed as he lost his footing, tumbled down to the creek and hit his head on a large lava rock.

Cal ran down the bank to his attacker and checked for a pulse.

"Is he dead?" he heard a voice from above. When Cal looked up, he was surprised to see Andy standing on the ridge.

"Yes, but I didn't kill him."

Andy nodded, "I know – I saw everything."

"What're you doing here?"

As Andy descended the bank, he said, "When I left the Double J, I drove past Gabe McNary's place and there was this Impala with stolen license plates." Andy saw Cal's look and added, "I checked…"

"So, you followed it," Cal said.

"Exactly. Who's this guy?"

Cal looked down at the dead body. "Badih Gaba, the man who killed Angel and caused the attack in Afghanistan where I lost the other two men on my team." He held up his cell phone and stopped the app. "I recorded it all."

"I'm just glad you're okay," Andy said and took out his phone to call the sheriff.

After he hung up, Andy looked at Cal and said, "So, you tried to put us off the scent about that coded message."

"You figured out Angel's message too?"

"Yep." Andy grinned. "You've gotta remember I was a history buff on everything about the world wars and the Enigma Machine was one of my passions. I figured since you had five men on your team, you'd most likely use that number instead of six."

CHAPTER 56

ANDY AND CAL WALKED into the sheriff's office. Morrow was talking to two men in military uniform. Cal recognized one of the men – his CO at Camp Lejeune. He didn't know the other man.

The sheriff said, "We will be releasing the first suspect we had on Angel Ramriez's case, as well."

"Major Morrison, sir," Cal said as he immediately straightened his posture. He was about to salute but remembered he was out of uniform and no longer in the military.

"Hello, Cal," the major said. He turned to the other officer next to him. "This is Lieutenant George Sanders."

Cal shook the man's hand and asked, "What're you two doing here?"

The major said, "We've been following the trail of Badih Gaba since there was a second attack in Afghanistan but lost track of him until we received your call about Angel Ramirez's murder, which led us here."

"Badih was just a local guy hired to work in the chow hall on our base when I was over there," Cal offered.

"We know," the lieutenant said. "That was the insurgent's cover."

The lieutenant looked at the major. "I guess we did need Cal's help after all."

"Excuse me?" Cal asked.

"Mistakenly, we thought we could handle this without you," Major Morrison said.

Andy stepped in. "I'm Detective Shaw and I was present when Cal encountered that man and I can vouch that Cal was defending himself. Mr. Gaba fell to his death during the struggle. It was all recorded on here." He handed Cal's cell phone to the sheriff.

"We'll make a copy for you," Sheriff Morrow said to the major.

Morrison smiled and nodded "That's how Cal was trained." Then he turned to the sheriff. "I understand Gaba's body has been taken to the local morgue."

"Yes, Major," the sheriff said.

The lieutenant stepped in. "We will escort the body back to our base for further arrangements."

The sheriff nodded.

"Then I think we are finished here," the major said.

A FEW MOMENTS LATER, Cal and the major were talking out in the parking lot.

"I've talked to Angel's family," Cal said, "and they want his body buried at Arlington with his other team members. I'd like to accompany his body, if possible."

"May I join you?" Major Morrison asked.

"I'd be honored, sir."

CHAPTER 57

"PRESENT ARMS," WAS CALLED out near the open gravesite in Arlington Cemetery.

Cal stood at attention in full dress uniform and saluted as he watched Angel's casket being carried to the burial site. The casket was then properly secured with a flag. Major Morrison stood at his side.

It was a sunny day in D.C., but the vast array of headstones against the white snow was more prevalent because of all the green wreaths with red bows. Cal had heard about the program where people could order winter wreaths for their fallen loved ones.

Angel's small family was seated nearby, his mother was in a wheelchair after a recent heart attack. Angel's younger brother stood next to his mother; his father had died two years prior.

After the chaplain finished the service, Cal knew that he was expected to make a speech. He walked up to the small podium at the head of the casket and said, "Corporal Angel Ramirez was a good man and a fine soldier. He was one of the bravest men I know and served his country honorably. Angel saved my life…"

During the military gun salute, all the men and women in uniform saluted. Cal thought of the three-shot meaning – duty, honor, and sacrifice and tears swelled in his eyes. Then the bugler played *Taps*. The casket team ceremoniously folded the flag and the leader presented it to Angel's mother. The chaplain gave his condolences to the family members and left.

CAL WAITED UNTIL MOST people left and Angel's body was lowered into the grave. Then, he walked to the headstones of the other three men of his team that he'd lost in that mission.

Major Morrison approached Cal. "Are you okay, son?"

"Yes, sir," Cal said as he fought back his tears. "I just wish that I had done a better job in keeping my men safe. I blame myself since I was their leader."

"Anyone who has been to battle always second guesses themselves afterward. You did nothing to cause that blast and you were one of the best team leaders I've had the pleasure to work with."

"But I could've done more for Angel."

After a moment of silence, the major looked skyward, then said, "What I've learned is that regret and blame help no one. As a survivor, we can only carry on the memories of those we've lost."

CHAPTER 58

SLUMPED ON THE COUCH in Micco's apartment, Cal sipped a beer as he watched his friend box up some of the photos and notes from their evidence board for Angel's murder.

"You look exhausted," Micco said.

"I'm bone tired."

Cal got up and took down Angel's photo from the board. "I've had this for so many years. It was taken when he joined my team…I just wish I'd reached out to him sooner." He laid the photo on the table near his beer and added, "But as the major told me, at some point, we have to learn to let go and move forward."

"Amen," Micco said as he put the box by his desk and joined Cal. The two drank beer in silence for some time.

Then, Cal smiled at his friend. "So, I think you and Hana make a great couple."

Micco rolled his eyes. "Couple? We've only been out on one date."

"Yes, but she's been such a great help on this case and it's adorable watching you two working together over your computers."

Smiling, Micco nodded. "She is amazing! I even find it hard to keep up with her."

"And beautiful."

Micco sighed. "Yeah, that, too."

"Maybe she could join our new team," Cal offered.

"I was hoping you'd say that!" Micco sipped his beer, then asked, "So, partner, what's next for the Triple-A Detective Service?"

"Did I tell you about why I went to Omaha on my flight home?"

"Nope. I figured you would when you're ready."

"I was looking into Jordan's parents' deaths. She has a different surname than her stepfather's and it's an unsolved case."

"Have you told Jordan about this yet?" Micco asked, raising his eyebrows.

"No, but I think this could be one of our next cases…"

THE END

ABOUT THE AUTHOR

This is Linda Kuhlmann's sixth novel – the second in the *Cal Jamison Murder Mystery Series*. Prior to this book, she wrote the *Koenig Triple Crown Series,* which began with a family mystery that evolved into a fictional portrayal of the horseracing underworld. She has also written an unrelated novel, *The Red Boots*, set in both Ireland and Oregon, and a small non-fiction booklet for Kindle called *Shameless Marketing for Writers*. Ms. Kuhlmann lives in Oregon.

Wreaths Across America website:
www.wreathsacrossamerica.org

Made in the USA
Monee, IL
06 January 2024